Books by K

A Rainey Daye Cozy Mystery Series

Pumpkin Spice Lies
A Pumpkin Hollow Mystery
By Kathleen Suzette

A Freshly Baked Cozy Mystery Series

A Gracie Williams Mystery Series
Pushing Up Daisies in Arizona,
A Gracie Williams Mystery, Book 1
Kicked the Bucket in Arizona,
A Gracie Williams Mystery, Book 2

A Home Economics Mystery Series
Appliqued to Death
A Home Economics Mystery, book 1

Table of Contents

Chapter One

I WALKED INTO THE KITCHEN at the candy store and stopped, inhaling deeply. The scent of a mixture of spices hung in the air. "Oh my gosh, that smells so good," I said.

Mom looked at me from where she stood at the counter, smoothing out a tray of fudge with the back of a wooden spoon. She smiled. "The first batch of the year of pumpkin spice fudge. It seems like forever since I made any, and I sure do miss it."

I went to stand beside her, looking at the huge tray of fudge she had made. "I miss it, too. There's nothing like pumpkin spice fudge." The cinnamon and clove scent brought back so many memories from Halloweens past. "I think I could eat this whole tray by myself."

"You and me both," she said with a grin. "Let's give it a few more minutes to set up, and then we'll have a taste."

My mouth watered. "I don't know if I can wait, but I'll try." If ever there was a scent that told the story of my life, it would have to be pumpkin spice.

"I recognize that wonderful smell," Christy said, suddenly appearing at the kitchen doorway. "I can smell it all the way over in the shop."

We had recently leased the smaller shop next door to the candy store and turned it into our kitchen so we could enlarge the candy shop and also make a break room for the employees. Beginning last year, we had had to hire temporary employees that worked during the busier seasons, so the break room had been a needed addition.

I turned to her. "Isn't it wonderful?"

She came to look at the fudge, and smelled it. "Oh, my gosh, I've got to have some now. Can I please have some pumpkin spice fudge?"

"Give it a few minutes to finish cooling," Mom said. "We'll all have some then."

Christy groaned.

Pumpkin Hollow is a small town in Northern California, and we celebrate Halloween all year long. The Halloween season runs from Labor Day weekend through about the second week of November, depending on when the second weekend of the month lands. But we had decided that having a mini Halloween season during the summer would do a lot to help local businesses. We dubbed the event Pumpkin Hollow Days, and it ran for two weeks in July. Tomorrow was the opening day of our second annual Pumpkin Hollow Days event, and the town was abuzz with excitement.

We weren't selling the pumpkin spice fudge online or in the store until tomorrow, and it would only be available for the two weeks that Pumpkin Hollow Days ran. It would make another appearance online and in the candy store during the Halloween season, and then be retired again after Thanksgiving. Pumpkin Hollow Days was our little tease until the Halloween season began.

"You should sell pumpkin spice fudge all year long," Christy said, smoothing a tiny bit of the fudge from the edge of the pan where it had spilled. She put it in her mouth and groaned. "So good."

"Absence makes the heart grow fonder, but since we're talking about candy, it makes the taste buds grow fonder," Mom said. "If we sell it all year long, it will become common and every day. It's special, and I want to keep it that way."

I knew what Mom meant, but I was pretty sure I could eat it every day and not grow tired of it.

The Pumpkin Hollow Candy Store was handed down from my mother's parents, and one day it would be handed down to Christy and me.

"I know," Christy relented. "I just love this stuff."

Mom chuckled and went to the cupboard and removed a knife and three small plates. "Me too. I guess it won't hurt if we don't wait."

She cut into one end of the fudge and put three small pieces on the plates and handed them to us.

"Yum," I said and took a bite of the still warm fudge. As I ate it, the swirl of spices filled my mouth, and I made a '0' with my thumb and forefinger. "Perfect."

"Do you think I put too much cloves in it?" Mom asked, smelling her piece.

I shook my head. "No. I love cloves. I wouldn't change a thing."

"It's wonderful," Christy agreed. "I swear, I could eat a pound of this every day."

"Me too," I said and finished the small piece. I looked longingly at the rest of the fudge in the pan. I could seriously eat a huge slab of it by myself.

"We already have fourteen walk-in orders for it," Mom informed us. "The locals know it's coming and they couldn't wait. I've got to get some more made. I think I'll leave the recipe as it is. Unless I decide to add more ginger later." She shrugged.

"Fourteen?" Christy asked. "On top of what you're making to take to the vendor fair tomorrow?"

She nodded. "People have been coming in for days now, placing orders for it."

"I don't blame them, but that's a lot of fudge to make today," I said. "I'm glad they can't order it online yet."

"Well, that changes tomorrow, so we've got to get working on it," Mom said as she measured out sugar for another batch.

"Hey, I knew I smelled something good coming from in here."

I turned and saw my fiancé, Detective Ethan Banks, standing in the doorway. "Doesn't it smell heavenly?"

He chuckled and came to stare at the pan of fudge. "Heavenly is the right word for it. How did I not know this was happening today?"

"I don't know. You weren't thinking," I said and brushed a lock of blond hair from his forehead. "We've got the vendor fair tomorrow, and Mom said she already has orders for pumpkin spice fudge waiting to be filled." I went to the cupboard and got him a plate.

"Can I put an order in?" he asked, looking at Mom.

"Of course you can," she said. "But there may be a little wait. How are you doing, Ethan?" She went to the refrigerator to get the butter out.

He nodded. "I'm doing great now that I'm getting some pumpkin spice fudge. I swear, the whole candy store smells like pumpkin spice. You're going to drive the customers crazy with it."

"Good, we'll sell a bunch of it," Mom said.

I cut him a piece that was larger than what Mom had given us, and put it on the plate and handed it to him. "Here you go."

He leaned over and kissed me and took the plate. "You're the best fiancée a guy could ever have."

I chuckled and felt myself blush. "You're so adorable," I said and hugged him.

"You two are sickeningly cute," Christy said dryly.

"We can't help it, it comes naturally," Ethan said and took a bite of his fudge.

I shrugged at her. "You and Devon are cute, too, so you can't say anything about us being too cute."

She smiled. "I'm going back out front to make sure everything is filled and straightened." She headed to the kitchen doorway.

"Well?" I asked Ethan.

He shook his head. "This is the best fudge I've ever eaten. Seriously. I love all the flavors you make, Ann, but this is the best, hands down."

My mother turned to him, carton of butter in hand. "Thank you, Ethan, that's kind of you to say. I think we're all partial to it. But I love hearing how much people enjoy the candy I make."

"I'll tell you how much I love it, as long as I get a lot of it."

She grinned and unwrapped a cube of butter.

"What are you up to?" I asked him.

He shrugged. "Not much. I just got a break in between doing paperwork and a meeting, and I thought I'd stop by and see what you were up to."

"I'm glad you stopped by. I have bad news, though."

His eyes widened. "What? How bad?"

I shrugged. "Kind of bad. I can't find a place to hold the wedding reception. I waited too long to find one. I'm sorry." I'd been worried about it for weeks as I called around to find a venue, and I didn't have any choice but to tell him now.

"What about the ballroom? I know you don't want to hold it there because of the murders, but it's a nice place." He finished his piece of fudge and eyed the tray.

"It's booked. The Baptist church has a recreation hall we could use, but it's small and stuffy. I don't want to do it there." It was my fault we didn't have a place to hold the reception. I hadn't gotten around to looking into it when like I should have.

His mouth made a straight line. "We'll have to come up with something."

"Why don't you have it in our backyard?" Mom suggested.

"Your backyard?" I asked, turning to her.

She nodded. "Sure, there's the gazebo back there, and you could rent some tables and chairs, and string some tiny clear lights in the trees. I think it would be sweet."

As she spoke, I suddenly pictured it. Mom and Dad had a large backyard, and the white wooden gazebo was sitting at the back of the yard. We could set tables with food beneath it, and string the tiny lights all over the yard. It would be beautiful. I looked at Ethan.

"What do you think?"

He grinned. "I think it would be perfect."

"I think so, too." I looked at Mom. "Let's do it. We weren't planning on having a fancy dinner anyway. We could set the food up buffet style, get some pretty centerpieces, and put everything together without any trouble."

She nodded. "Let's do it, then. We can come up with a lot of ideas to make it really pretty."

I breathed a sigh of relief. "Mom, you just solved all of my problems."

She smiled and shook her head as she turned the fire on beneath the saucepan. "I'm not a problem solver by calling, but I can do it when the pressure is on."

I chuckled and kissed Ethan. Mom and Dad's backyard would be perfect.

Chapter Two

AFTER ETHAN LEFT, CHRISTY and I set about cleaning the candy store and making sure all the shelves were filled. We had extended the front counter when we had moved the kitchen and there were new glass candy dispensers with wrapped candy on the extended front counter. Taffy, striped candy sticks, gumballs, and an assortment of gummy candies and licorice.

We'd also bought a few new decorations for the store, including a life-sized scarecrow that sat on a bale of straw, and a gigantic jack-o'-lantern with a happy grin that sat next to him. Clear twinkle lights were strung around the front window, and we put up fresh spider web in the corners. I glanced around the shop, making sure everything was ready and in its place.

"Looks pretty good, doesn't it?" Linda Reid asked as she came to stand beside me and look over the shop herself. Linda was one of our part-time employees, and a friend of my mother's who had proved to be an excellent addition to the staff.

"I think it does. I still need to stop by the gift shop and pick up some blackberry pie and pumpkin spice candles Polly got in.

We can burn them and make the place smell even tastier than it already does."

"Oh, blackberry pie candles? I might need to stop by there myself and pick up a few things for my house."

"They sound good, don't they? I want to put some on the front counter, and maybe put some here and there on the shelves." I stepped forward and straightened a fabric witch that was hanging precariously from a shelf.

"I can hardly wait for the Halloween season. Pumpkin Hollow Days are far too short for my tastes."

I smiled. "You're right. I still prefer the Halloween season. The weather is beautiful in the fall, and I get to wear sweaters and boots. We'll just call Pumpkin Hollow Days a dry run for the big show."

She chuckled and headed to the kitchen. "I'll see if your mother needs any help."

The bell over the door jingled, and I turned toward it. Mary Jones walked through the door and smiled at me. "Hi Mia," she said. "I was driving by, and I suddenly had a hankering for your mother's fudge."

"Well, you came to the right place then." I went back behind the counter while Mary stepped up to the display case.

"You all did some rearranging in here, didn't you? I guess I haven't been in here in a long while."

"We did. We took over the shop next door and turned it into our kitchen and made the shop a little bigger."

She looked around, her white curly hair bobbing with the motion. "Well, I like it. It gives you more room to put out more candy. That's a good thing." She chuckled.

"We thought it was a good idea with all the Internet sales we've been doing. We just didn't have enough room to pack and ship everything in our former kitchen."

She looked at me. "The world sure has changed since I was young. I guess just saying something like that makes me sound old." She chuckled and looked into the display case again.

"Nonsense. You're only as old as you feel."

She chuckled again. "The problem is, I feel old." She shrugged, grinning. "Oh well, I guess if I don't tell anyone, maybe they won't notice."

"That's right. With tomorrow being the start of Pumpkin Hollow Days, you get a chance to feel like a kid again. You can dress up and go trick or treating with the kids." On the last Saturday of Pumpkin Hollow Days, the kids would go trick or treating at the businesses. I could hardly wait.

She laughed again. "I have a feeling that will never happen. Do you have some of your mother's pumpkin spice fudge in yet?"

I eyed her. "Well, it's not supposed to be available until tomorrow, but if you promise not to tell anyone you got it early, I might be able to get you some. How much did you want?"

She grinned, holding her black purse in front of herself. "How about a quarter of a pound? I'd like to get more, but my doctor wouldn't approve of my finishing off a pound of fudge by myself."

"You got it." I picked up a cute white paper bag decorated with jack-o'-lanterns and headed to the kitchen. "I'll be right back."

Mom looked up at me as I entered the kitchen. "Everything all right out there, Mia?"

"Everything's great. Mary Jones came in and asked about pumpkin spice fudge. I told her I could sell her some as long as she didn't tell anyone she got it early."

Mom chuckled and kept stirring the fudge she was making. "I hope she can keep a secret."

I cut a piece of pumpkin spice fudge that looked to be the right size, then wrapped it, put it into the paper bag, and headed back out front.

"Here we are," I said and went behind the counter.

"Lovely. And why don't you give me some of those strawberry bonbons? Two of them, please."

"You got it."

I got her candy, and she paid for it and left. Christy came out of the break room, glancing at the wrought-iron clock on the wall above the door.

"I'm glad we're almost done here. I'm tired. What are you going to be tomorrow?"

"Well, I'm not going to wear anything with a cape. I learned my lesson last year. I'm going to stick with costumes that aren't very heavy." During Pumpkin Hollow Days, nearly everyone in town dressed up in costumes. I had made the mistake of wearing a little red riding hood costume last summer, and I had regretted it. The cape was far too heavy for summer. "I think I might be a female Waldo from Where's Waldo."

"That's a good idea."

"And it's easy," I said. "All I had to buy was a striped shirt."

Mom came out of the kitchen, untying her apron. "I think I'm about done for the day, girls. Oh, I meant to stop by Pumpkin Center Park and check on where our booth is located. I requested it to be beneath one of the trees to help keep the candy from melting, but I forgot to stop by to see if we got one there for sure."

"We can stop by on our way home," I offered. I had picked Christy up for work when her car didn't start, and the park wasn't too far out of the way.

"Would you? Today has been a long one for me. I meant to leave for home earlier, but I got sidetracked with the pumpkin spice fudge."

"It's no problem," I said.

I PULLED INTO THE PARKING lot at the park, and Christy and I got out. Mom had said we had booth number twenty-six. We headed down the sidewalk that meandered through the center of the park and glanced at the numbers on the tables.

"Looks like we must be someplace toward the back," Christy said.

I looked across the park. The park had been doing some construction, adding new park benches, playground equipment, and new covering for the grounds. There was still a backhoe parked near the swing set, and an area was taped off with yellow caution tape. I frowned.

"I hope they move that backhoe before tomorrow morning."

"Yeah, that doesn't look great. Maybe someone will move it in the morning."

We kept walking and found our booth not far from the playground. Thankfully, it was beneath a big cottonwood tree that provided shade past the edge of the booth.

"Looks good," I said, coming around the back of the booth to inspect it.

"Yeah," she said absently. "But I hate that we're so close to this end of the park. People are going to be parking at the other end."

"Yeah, but I bet it won't matter. They'll want to see everything, and they'll come all the way down here to see all the booths."

She was quiet for a moment. "Yeah, probably so."

There were another dozen booths on the other side of the playground. We were going to have a big turn out with local businesses, and some from out of town. It would bring some much needed revenue to the town, and I was excited about that.

"Hey, Mia," Christy said.

"Yeah?" I answered, looking at her over my shoulder. She was looking in the direction of the backhoe.

"What's that?"

I turned around and looked in the direction she was looking.

"What's what?"

"That," she said, pointing.

I wasn't sure what she was looking at. "What—" and then I saw it. We were both quiet.

"Doesn't that look odd?"

I nodded. It did look odd. Right in front of the backhoe was a suspicious-looking mound of dirt. Something about its shape gave me the chills. "Yeah, that is odd."

"Let's go see," Christy said, and started walking toward it.

I followed after her. "It's probably where they dug up the ground for the new playground equipment."

The city had been working on making improvements all over town in anticipation of the Halloween season, and there was some concern that the park wouldn't be finished before Pumpkin Hollow Days began, but it looked like they just needed to do a little touch-up work and they would be done.

"Yeah, probably."

We stood in front of the mound of dirt. Someone had tried to smooth it out, but its surface was still more than six inches above the rest of the ground.

"What do you think?" she asked me.

"I don't know."

I shrugged and stepped closer, then crouched down. There was something wrong about this mound of dirt.

"Mia?"

"Yeah?"

"What's that?"

I glanced at her and followed her gaze. There was something covered in dirt lying on top of the mound. When I got closer, it looked like an emerald ring. I reached for it, but when I tried to pick it up, it was stuck. I wiggled it, trying to make it come free. And that was when I screamed.

Chapter Three

THE FOLLOWING MORNING dawned clear and bright. The weatherman said it would be a hot one, and I wasn't looking forward to the heat. I was dressed as Waldo, substituting a long-sleeve T-shirt for the sweater, and I hurried to my car, casting a glance over my shoulder at Ethan's cottage across the street. His truck still wasn't parked in the driveway. Pulling my phone from my pocket, I saw it was just after six a.m. An image came to mind of the ring I had tried to pick up from the mound of dirt at the park the previous evening, and it made me shudder. There had been a hand attached to it.

I drove over to the Little Coffee Shop of Horrors and went inside. Brian was behind the counter and he gave me a sleepy grin.

"Hey, Mia. Fancy meeting you here this early."

I forced myself to smile. "You look like you didn't sleep well." I had dated Brian in high school and now he was married to my best friend. Sometimes life takes a turn, and it really is for the best.

He shook his head. "Isabella isn't cooperating."

I chuckled. Brian and Amanda had just had their first baby, and she was just over a month old. Sleep was a precious commodity for the two of them.

"I bet. But she's so darn adorable, it totally makes up for it."

He nodded, grinning. "She sure is. I still can't get over the fact that I'm a father. I mean, we have a baby." He shook his head. "Who knew that becoming a father was the best thing in the world?"

I chuckled. "She is pretty amazing. Little Isabella is one lucky baby, with parents like you and Amanda."

Brian blushed. He was dressed as Dracula, and I thought he would regret the cape if he had to spend much time outside today. "Thanks, but I think we're the lucky ones. That baby is the most perfect baby I've ever seen."

"You can say that again." I grinned and glanced up at the order board. "How about you make me a bloody vampire, a vanilla mummy, and then—oh, why don't you make me seven vanilla mummies?"

"You got it. Is Ethan with you?" He glanced at my car parked at the curb.

I shook my head. "No, he had a late night. Why don't you add an extra shot of espresso to the bloody vampire? I think he could use it right about now." The bloody vampire was a raspberry mocha, and I knew Ethan would appreciate it. Not to mention he probably needed the extra caffeine right about now.

He picked up a cup. "You bet. So he had a late night?" he asked as he got to work on the coffees.

"Yeah." I glanced over my shoulder, but the coffee shop was empty. "Christy and I found a body at the park."

His eyes widened. "Really? Who was it?"

I shrugged. "I have no idea. Whoever it was, they were buried."

"Wow. At the park? The night before Pumpkin Hollow Days begin?"

I nodded. "I don't know what's going to happen with the vendor's fair. Hopefully, Ethan has done all the investigating he needs to do, and the fair can go on as planned."

He squirted whipped cream onto the bloody vampire. "Yeah, that would be a shame if it had to be canceled."

"Don't say that. We've all been looking forward to this. My mother has made a lot of extra candy. In fact, she should be at the candy store making some more right now." I glanced at my phone again, then looked at the display case of baked goods. There were three kinds of scones. "I hate to clean you out, but why don't you give me eight scones? Any flavors."

"You got it," he said as he continued working on the coffees.

"Who's doing all your baking now that Amanda is taking some time off?" Amanda was the baker at the shop, and she was in no hurry to go back to work with little Isabella at home.

He grinned. "That would be me. She watched me do it for a few weeks before turning me loose. I think I've turned into a pretty good baker."

"That's awesome. That means she can put you to work in the kitchen indefinitely."

His brow furrowed. "No, thanks. I might be good at it, but it isn't my favorite thing to do."

"Suit yourself," I said with a shrug.

When Brian finished making the coffees, he put them into two cardboard carriers and put the scones into smaller bags, and then all of them went into a larger bag. I paid for everything and hurried out to my car. On my way to the park, I dropped most of the coffee and scones off at the candy store. I kept one coffee for Ethan, and one for myself and brought two scones with me.

I PARKED ON THE SIDE of the park that was closest to the playground area. The police had set up a chain-link barricade that they had covered with tarps so no one could see what was happening on the other side. I breathed out and steeled myself as I walked around the side of the barricade.

Ethan was talking to a uniformed officer. He smiled tiredly at me when he saw me.

"Hey," I said, approaching him. The officer left, and I handed Ethan a coffee and a scone. "I thought you might need these."

"You have no idea," he said and kissed me. He took a sip of his coffee and then sighed.

"Good?"

He nodded. "Excellent. I so needed this."

"You've been here all night?" I asked, glancing at the mound of dirt that was now a shallow hole. Thankfully, whoever had been in the makeshift grave had already been removed.

"I went home for a couple of hours of sleep, and came back a little over an hour ago. I got some coffee at the gas station, but let's just say it isn't the best coffee around."

"I bet." I glanced at the hole again. "Do you know who it is?" I whispered.

He shook his head. "No. She looked familiar, but we'll have to wait until we identify her."

That didn't sound promising. "Had she been there long?"

"I don't think so. Hard to say at this point. We talked to the construction crew, and they were here Thursday afternoon, so we can narrow down the time frame."

I sighed. "That's so sad. Did you see anything that might be helpful to the case when you uncovered her?"

He looked at me. "It's too early yet to know much yet. I know you want the details, but I don't have many right now. I guess you're going to have to wait." He grinned, and then took a big sip of his coffee. "This is so good."

"I had Brian add a shot of espresso to it. I figured you could use the caffeine."

"You figured right."

There were dark circles beneath his eyes, but the coffee made him look more awake now. "So this won't interfere with the vendors' fair?" I asked, glancing back at the barricade. It would be a couple of hours before people began arriving to set up, with the fair beginning at ten o'clock.

He shook his head. "I don't think so. We'll have officers posted at both ends of the barricade, and add on some more length to the sides to keep people out of the area, but as long as we don't tell people what's going on, I think we'll be fine.

With the construction work that's been going on, people will probably just think it's more work being done and they just want to keep visitors out of it."

I nodded. "That's a good idea." I sighed. "I'm kind of creeped out by seeing that hand when I tried to pick up the ring."

"I don't blame you. That's kind of a scary thing to have happen."

I glanced at the evidence markers on the ground. "Did you find anything important?"

"Maybe. There were some shoe prints and a barrette. But the barrette looked like a kid's, not a woman's."

I turned to him. "What did it look like?"

"It had a white poodle on it. Plastic. It kind of looked old. Not that it was in bad condition, but that it looked like an old-style I've seen somewhere before. I just can't remember where."

"Vintage, you mean?"

He nodded. "Yeah. It seems like I've seen one like it around somewhere."

"Was it an older woman?" I asked. I couldn't imagine a kid's barrette being left at a crime scene when there wasn't a child victim.

"No, actually, she looked young. Maybe as young as a teenager. But until we can get her identified, we won't have a lot of information." He looked into the bag. "I love pumpkin spice scones."

"I know you do," I said. Six officers were milling about and talking. "I guess I could have called you and asked how many officers were here and gotten them a coffee."

He waved the thought away. "Mike just went to pick some coffee up. Don't worry about it. He's going to get me one, too, so now I'll have two. And boy do I need it."

I chuckled. "Are you going to have some free time to enjoy the vendors' fair?"

"I already filed my initial report, and I'm going to be leaving here in a half-hour or so. With a few more hours of sleep, I should be able to come back and see what's going on. Maybe."

I nodded. "Good. I don't want you to miss it. So have you had much time to think over having the wedding reception in my parent's back yard?"

He shrugged. "Honestly, I haven't thought about it since your mother brought it up, but I think it's a great place to have it. Why? Are you okay with it?"

I nodded. "I think it will be nice. I just didn't want you to feel like you had to go along with it just because my mother offered."

He smiled. "I think it's going to be really nice. As long as you like it, then I say we do it."

I nodded. "I can't wait."

Our wedding was coming together nicely, and I was excited about it. I glanced at the open hole where the woman was taken from, and I shivered. I hoped it wasn't a teenager. Some parents in Pumpkin Hollow might be waiting for a dreaded phone call as we spoke.

Chapter Four

"HI MIA, I SEE YOUR mom made pumpkin spice fudge," Polly Givens said.

I looked up at her from where I was setting sample trays out onto our booth table. "Hi, Polly." I nodded. "She did it. She finally made pumpkin spice fudge again, and it is delicious. And I'm not just saying that because she's my mom."

Polly was dressed as Morticia Addams from the Addams family. With her tall, thin build and long black hair, she had the natural looks to go with the outfit. She owned the gift shop and almost always dressed as Morticia during the Halloween season.

"Oh, I know you aren't just saying that. She has my vote for the best candy-maker on earth." Her eyes went over the candy on the glass-covered display plates. There were ice chests stashed beneath the booth table with more candy, and we'd take orders for whatever we ran out of.

"It turned out hot today," I said and took a sip of my iced tea. Christy had made a run to the local burger joint and bought us iced tea.

She looked at me and nodded. "That's the one drawback to having Pumpkin Hollow Days in the summer. The heat. But that's all right. We'll survive. And I got some new candles in, so if you get a minute, pop over to my booth and see what I've got."

"I will. You know I can't resist candles. Maybe I should have gone into business making them."

She chuckled. "I'd buy them from you to sell in my shop. But for now, how about I place an order for a pound of pumpkin spice fudge? I know your mom has been working her fingers to the bone making candy, so she can let me know when she gets it done next week, and I'll stop by the candy store and pick it up. No rush."

"Thanks, Polly. Mom will appreciate an order she doesn't need to make right away." I picked up a blank order form and began filling it out for her.

"I think I'll take this piece you have here, so at least I get a little taste of it right now," she said, indicating a quarter-pound slice beneath the glass cover.

"You got it." I finished filling out the form and got the piece of fudge for her and took her money for it. "I'll try to stop by your booth in just a bit."

She nodded absently, her eyes going to the barricade nearby. "What's going on over there?"

I glanced at it. "They've been working on the playground for a while now." I hated not telling Polly the truth. She was a friend, but I didn't feel right saying anything just yet. Someone's loved one had been found in that hole behind the barricade, and it would be awful for them to find out about it from someone other than the police.

She glanced at the barricade, and then nodded again. "Well, thanks for the fudge. I'll see you later."

"See you," I said.

Christy returned from the candy store with another ice chest of candy and set it down in the booth. "There. That should hold us for a while."

I sighed and picked up my Styrofoam cup of iced tea and took a sip. "I'm ready for fall weather. I am not a fan of the heat."

"Me too," she said, wiping the sweat from her forehead.

It didn't get as hot here in the mountains as it did in other parts of California, but each summer, we had a period that warmed up, and this was it.

Christy glanced at the barricade and sat down next to me. "Anything new on who was buried back there?"

I shook my head. "Not a word. Ethan said he would stop by the booth today. Maybe he'll know something then."

She nodded. "Seems like someone should have reported someone missing."

"You would think so. But maybe they weren't dead long when we found them, or maybe they were scheduled to go someplace this weekend, and their family hasn't even missed them yet."

"Wonder what would happen if we slipped back behind the barricade?" she asked, eyeing the formation.

"The police would stop you from being nosy. I saw Officer Chu hanging out around there."

She brushed back her long brown hair and turned to me. "Ethan needs to get us the details. How can we investigate without details?"

I chuckled. "Have patience, sister. He'll give us the details. Or at least, enough of them to start snooping." Ethan wasn't fond of us looking around and asking questions, but he had become resigned to the fact that it was going to happen whether he wanted it to or not.

I looked up as Angela Karis from the Sweet Goblin Bakery approached us. She was dressed as a cupcake, the costume covering her torso, and her head popped out from the fabric frosted top. The costume looked bulky and hot.

"That's a cute costume," Christy said, eyeing her.

Angela frowned, putting her hands where her hips should be. "Do you like it?" She glanced down at herself.

Christy hesitated. "It's unique."

Angela's lips curled. "Yeah, I'm not much of a seamstress." Her eyes went to the candy on the table. She sighed loudly. "I don't need more sugar, but I'll take a quarter-pound of pumpkin spice fudge." She nodded at the plate, then eyed me. "This has been one heck of a week."

"Oh?" I asked as Christy got the fudge for her.

She nodded, sighing again. "I didn't think I'd ever get this costume finished. I poked myself with a sewing needle at least four hundred times, and had to remove every seam. Twice. I don't know what I was thinking. Vince said I was nuts for making it, but I'm proud that I actually finished it."

I nodded. Vince Moretti owned the bakery, and Angela had been a friend of his now-deceased wife. A lot of people around town had suspicions about their relationship before Stella had died, and now that Vince and Angela were living together, their suspicions were confirmed. "I'm sure it was a lot of work. It's cute, though."

She nodded absently, her eyes on the candy again. "And then my sister called me in a panic late last night when my niece didn't come home the night before." She shook her head and looked at me now. "Between the three of us, the girl has always been a little wild. I don't know why my sister is getting excited about it anyway, she's eighteen. She has a right to stay out as long as she wants. But my sister was a blubbering mess when she called and kept me on the phone until nearly one o'clock in the morning." She yawned.

It took everything in me not to look at Christy. I could feel her looking at me, but I didn't want to give myself away, so I kept my eyes on Angela.

"Oh? Who is your niece?" I asked.

"Hailey Strong. Sweet girl. But she likes to push the limits. Everyone's limits." She chuckled heartily. "I bet the teachers were thrilled when she graduated from high school last year. Wouldn't surprise me if they passed her just to get rid of her."

"Really?" I asked carefully. "So she was in trouble a lot?"

"How about I get some of those cherry chocolate creams? They sure sound good." She pointed at a plate and Christy reached beneath the table to get some out of the ice chest.

"How many would you like?" she asked and looked at me. She squinted her eyes and nodded, trying to get something over to me. I turned away. I didn't want Angela to read anything on my face.

"Oh, how about a half dozen? I shouldn't get them, but I will. You know how I am." She turned to me. "I wouldn't say

Hailey was in trouble a lot at school. It's just that Hailey is a firecracker. She likes to pull practical jokes on people and she tends to be loud." She grinned. "I love that girl. But my sister is a worrywart. Always has been. Our father always said Jenny would worry herself to death one day. Wouldn't surprise me if he was right about that."

I smiled back and hoped Hailey was just off having some fun somewhere and wasn't in the county morgue. I needed to talk to Ethan and see if he had found out anything about the victim's identity.

"Did she try calling her?" I asked. "I'm a bit of a worrier myself, and I do know it's hard when someone you love doesn't show up where they're supposed to be." This time I did look at Christy. There was a time when she was out of pocket more than in.

Christy rolled her eyes at me.

"Oh sure, she called her. Wouldn't surprise me if she called her a hundred times last night. She needs to accept the fact that Hailey is an adult now and needs to live her life."

Christy handed her a cute Halloween decorated paper bag with her candy in it. "Some people have a hard time letting their kids grow up."

She nodded. "You can say that again." She paid for her candy and looked at me. "Well, if you get a hankering for a cupcake or a cookie, I've got a booth just down the sidewalk there."

"We just might have to go over and see what you've got," I said.

"See you, girls," she said and headed over to the next booth.

Christy and I turned to look at each other.

"I have a feeling about that."

"Me too." I picked up my cup and took a sip of my iced tea.

Chapter Five

MY BLACK CAT, BOO, rubbed up against my legs as I stood at my front window watching for Ethan. Ethan and I lived in matching cottages. There were six on my side of the street and six on his. They were white with black shutters and were all neatly kept. They were small, but they were the perfect size for a single person. I wasn't sure what we were going to do once we got married. The idea had occurred to me to find a larger house to rent until we decided on one to buy, but I enjoyed living in my little cottage and I didn't know if I was ready to give it up yet.

I glanced at the clock over my fireplace mantle. It was after eight o'clock in the evening and it was beginning to get dark. The vendors' fair had been a smashing success, with a lot of tourists showing up. We'd taken a lot of orders for candy and sold everything we had made earlier in the morning. I was beat, but I didn't want to go to bed without seeing Ethan. When Ethan didn't show up for the vendors' fair, it had taken all I had not to text or call him. But I knew he was busy, plus I had my hands full with the candy sales.

I bent over and scratched Boo's ear. "What do you think, Boo? Are you ready for the Halloween season?"

We would have a few weeks of down time in between Pumpkin Hollow Days and the Halloween season, and I was already looking forward to it. Ethan and I had taken a trip up to Lake Tahoe several weeks earlier, and I was wishing we had had more time before we had to come back to our jobs. We were still debating on where we would go for our honeymoon. Ethan wanted Hawaii, and I wanted Paris. My trip was a lot more expensive, but it was someplace I'd always wanted to go to. If we waited, we might never make the trip.

Ethan pulled into his driveway ten minutes later and I hurried out front. I hated to nag at him, but I needed to know the details.

"Hey," I said, looking both ways before crossing the street.

He turned and looked at me, smiling tiredly. "Hey yourself," he said, and when I got to him, he kissed me.

"You put in a long day."

He nodded. "I did. But you know how it goes."

"I sure do. Have you eaten?"

He looked at me, one eyebrow raised. "If you count a bag of chips and a soda from the vending machine at the police department, then yes. I've eaten."

"No, I don't call that eating. I call that snacking. I ordered a pizza earlier, it's cold now, but we can warm it up."

He took me by the hand and we headed back across the street. "I like cold pizza. Don't even bother sticking it in the microwave."

"You got it," I said, and we headed inside.

"Hi Boo," he said, and stopped to bend over and pet him. Boo meowed and rubbed up against his legs. "Sorry I didn't make it to the vendors' fair. Things were crazy."

"I figured as much. I wish you would have gotten to stop by, but I understand. So," I said, going to the kitchen and taking the pizza out of the refrigerator. I'd ordered it on a whim, and as soon as I placed the order I wished I'd waited until Ethan came home so we could eat together while it was still hot. "How are things going? Do you know who the victim is yet?"

He nodded and went to the cupboard and pulled out two glasses. "You have iced tea?"

"Of course," I said, and got the pitcher of tea out of the refrigerator and filled both glasses.

"It's Hailey Strong."

I turned and looked at him. "Hailey Strong? Angela Karis' niece?"

He nodded. "I think so. Her mother came into the police department early this morning and wanted to fill out a missing person's report. I asked her a few questions, and she showed me a picture of her that she had on her phone, and I was 99% sure that she was our victim. Then we matched up dental records to make sure. She had just had her teeth capped, and it was a perfect match."

I sighed and took two plates down from the cupboard and put them on the table. "What a shame. I saw Angela earlier today, and she thought Hailey's mother was overreacting to her not coming home the night before." I set the pizza on the table and we sat down with our iced tea.

He nodded and helped himself to the pizza, placing two slices on his plate. "I hated to tell her that her daughter was dead, with her being as young as she was. It's just a shame when a life that young is cut short."

"I can imagine that must have been difficult, talking to her mother like that," I said and took a sip of my iced tea. "Any ideas what happened to her? Do you know how she died yet?"

He shook his head. "We've got to wait on the report from the medical examiner. There wasn't any obvious trauma to the body. So until we hear from him, we won't know for sure. Her mother was crushed, as you can imagine."

I nodded again. "How horrible. Does she have any ideas about what might have happened to her?"

He chewed and swallowed a bite of pizza before answering. "Not really. She was so distraught it was hard to get much of anything out of her. I'm going to talk to her again in the morning."

I took a piece of pizza from the box and laid it on my plate. It'd been a couple of hours since I'd eaten and the pizza was so good I couldn't resist. "Angela Karis said that her niece was a practical joker. She described her as the life of the party."

One eyebrow shot up. "The life of the party? I wonder if the emphasis is on party?"

I shook my head. "I really don't know. She didn't elaborate on whether she was prone to partying. But she did mention that the high school was probably glad that she had graduated and maybe just passed her to get rid of her. I don't know how serious she was."

He smiled. "Well, that does paint a picture, doesn't it?"

I nodded. "Sure does. I wonder if Hailey had some sketchy party friends and something went wrong, and she ended up dead."

"That's probably a pretty good bet," he said and took another bite of his pizza. Boo rubbed up against his legs, begging for a taste.

I looked under the table at him. "Boo, you don't need any pizza. You had some ham off of mine earlier."

"Oh, but Mom," Ethan said, handing a piece of ham to Boo. He looked at me and smiled. "How could I not give him a piece?"

I rolled my eyes at him. "You are something else. The two of you are going to be quite a pair when we move in together."

"Don't forget about Licorice." He took a sip of his iced tea. "She won't appreciate being left out."

"Of course not. I'm sure Licorice will be right there in the middle of all the trouble the two of you will be getting into."

Ethan had his own black cat named Licorice. She was a more recent arrival than Boo. I had taken Boo in when he hung around the cottages looking for a home, and Licorice had come to Ethan after an earlier murder investigation.

We sat and visited as we finished our pizza, and then Ethan leaned back in his chair, placing his napkin on his empty plate. "So, how many days is it until we get married?"

I shook my head at him. "I haven't counted. Why? Are you getting anxious?"

He grinned. "Of course I'm getting anxious. Never in my life did I think that I would be anxious about getting married.

And I mean anxious to *get* married. But I'm ready to hang up my bachelor days and put them behind me."

I grinned. "Good. Say goodbye to those single bachelor days, because you are done with them."

He chuckled. "And you're done with your bachelorette days."

I rolled my eyes. "Yeah, you know I was a wild bachelorette. It will be so tough leaving that lifestyle behind."

He picked up his glass of tea and drained it. "Good. I don't want you looking back. From here on out, we're looking forward. To our married life together and to our future children." He set his empty glass on the table.

I raised my glass of iced tea and took a sip, then set it down. "Here's to the future. Our future together, and our future children, and our future home. Have you thought about that? Where are we going to live after we get married?"

He shrugged. "I thought you were moving into my house."

"That's a negative. I like my house better."

"Why? They're identical."

"I know, but I did some really cute decorating in my house, and you haven't done much of anything to yours. I think you own fewer things than I do anyway, it'll be easier to move you over here."

He shook his head. "You could just decorate over there."

I shook my head now. "No. You're moving in with me. And one of these days, after we save up a hefty down payment, we'll move into our own forever home."

He nodded. "It's a deal."

I was still having a hard time accepting the fact that this was really happening. I was going to marry Ethan Banks, the love of my life. But I figured I'd get used to it.

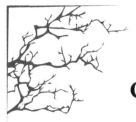

Chapter Six

MONDAY MORNING CHRISTY and I walked down to the Sweet Goblin Bakery. I hoped Angela would be there, but after losing her niece, it wouldn't have surprised me if she wasn't at work.

I pushed open the door to the bakery and inhaled the sweet scent of vanilla and donuts. Angela was finishing up with a customer at the front counter, and Christy and I walked up to the display case and peered in.

"Oh, she made muddy ghosts," Christy said.

I nodded. "She makes the best muddy ghosts." A muddy ghost was a Boston cream donut. Angela had a way with them that made them the best I'd ever tasted.

I glanced at Angela as she chatted for a moment with the woman at the front counter. Then I looked back at the display case. "And I love her decorated sugar cookies. She always does such a wonderful job." Angela had frosted the sugar cookies and drawn in Halloween scenes by hand with food coloring and icing.

"I've got to have that jack-o'-lantern sugar cookie." Christy moved down the display case. "Oh, she's got her boo berry donuts made."

I nodded, my eyes still on Angela. When her customer left, she turned toward us and forced herself to smile. "Hello girls," she said quietly. "I suppose you've heard?"

I nodded, clutching my purse to my side. I had dressed as a ballerina today and my black boho bag was out of place. "Angela, I'm so sorry. I hated to hear about what happened to your niece."

She looked down at her hands for a moment, then looked up at me. "I tell you, that girl was a firecracker. From the day she was born, she was the happiest baby I'd ever seen. She loved ballet, she loved any kind of dancing really, and she wanted to be an artist." Tears sprang to her eyes and her nose wrinkled up as she tried to keep them from falling.

I stepped up to the front counter. "I'm so sorry, Angela. I can't imagine how hard this is for you and your family."

She inhaled deeply. "Never in a million years would I have thought I would live to see the death of one of my nieces or nephews. You always think about the younger generation outliving you. But I sure was wrong about that."

I nodded. "How is your sister doing?"

She sighed. "The poor thing. Like I said, she's always been a worrier. And now her worst worry has come true, and she's beside herself. She blames herself, of course. I told her that was ridiculous. She had nothing to do with this. Her husband is a mess, too."

"Why would your sister blame herself?" I asked. Christy came to stand beside me.

"It's just that worrying tendency she has. Somehow self-blame just feeds itself into those thoughts. She was that way with both of her kids; always worried she wasn't a good enough mother. That maybe she wasn't doing enough to keep them safe or healthy." She shook her head. "I never had any kids, so I didn't have to deal with those sorts of worries, but I always thought she went a little overboard with it. But, I guess unless you have kids of your own, it's hard to know if a parent is going overboard or not."

"I think I remember Hailey from when I was a teacher's aide at the elementary school years ago," Christy said. "It was my first real grown-up job; I was eighteen when I started work there. It was so much fun working with the fifth-grade class. And if I remember right, Hailey was the happiest child there. A little distracted, but it seemed like she was always laughing."

Angela beamed. "That was her all right. She laughed all the time. I just don't know what the family is going to do without her. When I went to sleep last night, I swear I could hear her laugh echoing in my mind." She shook her head sadly and wiped a tear away.

Angela was about to make me cry with her. She spoke so fondly of her niece, that I could just picture it. I wasn't sure that I had ever met Hailey, but the way that she described her, I felt like I knew her.

"Angela, do you have any idea what might have happened to her?" I asked.

She looked at me solemnly for a moment. "I really don't, except that I know she had boyfriend troubles."

Now we were getting somewhere. "Oh? What kind of boyfriend troubles?"

She put both her hands on the front counter and glanced at the closed door. We were the only customers in the shop.

"She was dating Joey Harper. You know him?"

I thought about it a moment. "I think I do know him. Doesn't he work at the shoe store?"

She nodded. "Yes, he's worked there for a couple of years. He was still in high school when he started. He worked a few hours each day after school. But the last time I talked to Hailey, she told me the two of them were fighting. I didn't think a lot of it at the time, but now that I think things over, I have to wonder about him."

"Did she say anything specifically?" I asked, glancing at the donuts in the display case. I had promised to bring a box of donuts back to the candy store. Mom, Carrie, and Linda were making candy to fill the orders we had taken over the weekend at the vendors' fair.

"She said he was crazy jealous, and she was tired of it. They were arguing all the time, I guess. He thought she was flirting with another boy, but she swears up and down that she never did anything like that."

"Was there a specific boy that she mentioned?" I asked.

She nodded. "Yes, Matt Edwards. I'm not sure I know him though."

"Did she say why her boyfriend thought she was flirting with him?" Christy asked, leaning on the front counter.

"Apparently he gave her a ride home from college last May. She said it was a warm day, and she'd stayed after class to get some help with an assignment. She'd been struggling with her schoolwork and she had been worried about her grade." She chuckled dryly. "Hailey always struggled a little in school. If you ask me, it was because she was so sociable with all the other kids." She shook her head and chuckled again. "That was the way she was. Just so full of energy."

"Sometimes kids have trouble with school if they're the talkative type," I said.

"She certainly was. My sister and I were talking about her one night recently and wondering when she would settle down to get married. Her mother wanted her to get married right away because she wanted grandkids." She rolled her eyes but chuckled when she said it. "I told her that Hailey needed to take her time and wait until she grew up a little more. Hailey's silliness showed her immaturity, and I didn't want to see her marry someone just because she wanted to get married. I wanted her to wait and do a little more growing up."

I nodded. "Do you know anything else about Joey Harper?" I asked.

She shook her head. "I really don't. I wish I did, and I'm thinking I might go over to the shoe store and talk to Joey and see if he knows anything about who might have killed her."

I glanced at Christy. "Maybe you should let the police handle that. If you're worried that he may have had something to do with her death, you might just want to talk to Ethan about it and let him handle things."

She looked at me, her eyes widening. "Well, I guess I didn't think about it that way. I just can't imagine who would do that to my poor niece. I mean, they killed her and buried her at the park. That doesn't even make sense."

I nodded. "Murderers seldom think things through. It seems like most murders are committed on the spur of the moment. It may be that they just happened to see that equipment there at the park and buried her there."

She nodded. "And there aren't any cameras turned on at that part of the park. Can you believe it? There are some around the restrooms, the parking lot, and the snack bar that they use when they have events at the park, but none on the playground. It doesn't make sense to me."

"That doesn't make sense," Christy agreed. "I would think they would want a camera on the playground in case someone has an accident, or in case, well, a crime is committed."

She nodded and sniffed. "I'm sure Ethan will sort things out and arrest the killer. Well girls, what can I get for you today?" She brightened as she said it, but I knew it was just an act.

"We promised we'd bring a dozen donuts back to the candy store for everyone," I said, looking at the display case that held the donuts. "They all look so good.

"They are," she said. "If I'm may say so myself."

I grinned. "Why don't you get me three of your boo berry donuts, three muddy ghosts, three old-fashioned witches, and three pumpkin spice."

"And one more for a baker's dozen?"

I nodded. "A green goblin."

She unfolded the bakery box and opened the back of the display case. "I'm sure Ethan will find her killer," she repeated. "I still can't get over the fact that she's dead. It was only a couple of weeks ago that I last spoke to her."

"So did she say if she and her boyfriend had broken up?" Christy asked as she watched Angela filling the box with donuts. "You said that they were arguing a lot. Did she mention them breaking up?"

Angela stopped, a pumpkin spice donut in her hand, and looked at her, thinking. "You know, I don't recall whether she said that or not. She just said they were arguing a lot, so I assumed they were still together, just not getting along very well."

Christy nodded. "Makes you wonder if they broke up or not."

"I wish she had. Maybe she would still be alive."

I felt bad for Angela and her family. It had to be crushing to lose someone who was still so young and had so much life ahead of them yet. Christy and I would do what we could on our end to discover whatever information we could, and hopefully it would help Ethan in his search for the killer.

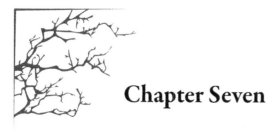

Chapter Seven

"I HOPE YOU'RE READY for donuts," I said to Mom, Linda, and Carrie. They were working away in the kitchen, each of them making a different flavor of fudge.

Mom turned to look at us. "Donuts? I don't mind if I do."

I took the box of donuts and set them on the counter and opened the box up. The scent of donuts rose into the air, and for a moment drowned out the scent of fudge. Christy set two cardboard carriers with cups of coffee next to the donuts.

"We stopped by Amanda's and got some coffee, too," she said. "Vanilla mummies and pumpkin spice lattes."

"Oh," Linda said, turning to look. "Pumpkin spice?"

I nodded. "Brian decided that they had to have pumpkin spice lattes during Pumpkin Hollow Days. I told him that was an excellent idea."

She nodded and hurried over, looking at the cups of coffee in the carriers. "You can say that again. I love pumpkin spice everything. But then, who doesn't?"

"Only crazy people don't like pumpkin spice everything," Christy said, taking a step back and looking at me. "Maybe we should have gotten all pumpkin spice lattes."

"I'll take a vanilla mummy," Mom said, coming over and picking up a cup of coffee. "With all the pumpkin spice fudge I've been eating, the vanilla will cleanse my palate." She chuckled.

"Good, because I want a pumpkin spice latte," I said. "We only got two vanilla mummies." We had bought two extra coffees in case somebody wanted another one later, or for when Sarah and Lisa came into work later.

I glanced around the kitchen. It looked like Mom had been busy since she had gotten in at four o'clock in the morning. I'd offered to come in when she did and help, but she had opted to have me and Christy come in a little later so there would be more coverage for the shop when we opened.

"We got so many orders for fudge over the weekend," Mom said, taking a sip of her coffee. "We're going to be busy these next two weeks."

"We'll be busy until after Valentine's Day," Christy corrected her. "Honestly, we've just got a few weeks between Pumpkin Hollow Days and the Halloween season, and I bet things don't slow down at all."

Mom nodded and took another sip of her coffee. "Oh, this is good. But you're right, Christy, there probably won't be a slowdown in business at all. Except for the fact that we won't have pumpkin spice fudge for a few weeks in between, I'm sure things will be jumping until after Valentine's Day."

"I can hardly wait for the Halloween season," Linda said and picked out a boo berry donut. "But I'm really looking forward to Christmas. There's just something about all the snow on the ground and the Christmas decorations that I can't get enough of. Sometimes I wish Pumpkin Hollow had been Christmas Hollow or something like that." She chuckled.

"That's a great idea," Mom said. "Maybe we could do both a Halloween theme and a Christmas theme at the same time all year long?"

Christy groaned. "No, don't say that. We've got too much work as it is. And now that I think about it, how are things going with finding the temporary employees?"

Mom had decided to hire more temps for the next few months. We had done the same thing last year, and it had worked out well. Mom was hoping to be able to hire the same ladies since they had already been trained.

"I called three of them and they are excited about starting back to work. Barbara said she had been going stir crazy and was just about to give me a call and see if we needed any extra help."

"Great," I said, grabbing an old-fashioned witch donut and a napkin. "I'm glad we'll have people that are already trained. That will make things go smoothly."

I glanced at the clock on the wall and saw it was nearly time to open the shop. "I'll go out front and get things opened up."

"All right, dear," Mom said.

I straightened my tutu and went into the candy shop. I was excited about all the improvements we had made to the store when we took over the shop next door, making the kitchen larger and the shipping and receiving as well as the shop itself.

It made everything so much easier. I glanced around. We had bought some new decorations over the weekend. There were paper mâché pumpkins scattered among the shelves and a large felt ghost stood grinning in one corner and a light up plastic jack-o-lantern sat next to it.

"Looks pretty good, doesn't it?" Christy said from behind me as she followed me into the shop.

I nodded, still taking everything in. "It sure does. I just love this candy shop. Especially during the holidays. I think we must have the best job in the world."

She nodded and went back behind the front counter and set her coffee down. "I'm not going to argue with you there."

I went over to the front door and unlocked it, then came back and joined Christy behind the counter. I looked up as the bell over the door jingled, and Polly walked through it. She stopped and inhaled. "Oh my gosh, chocolate and vanilla, and everything that's sweet and yummy."

"Isn't it the best smell ever?" I asked.

"I can't get enough of it myself," Christy said.

She nodded and came up to the front counter. "I'm not here to put any pressure on your mother to make that pound of pumpkin spice fudge I ordered the other day, but that little piece that I got there at the vendors' fair just wasn't enough to hold me." She looked at the display case. "Can I get another quarter pound?"

"Of course you can," I said. "How did you do over the weekend? Did you sell a lot?" I opened up the display case and took out the tray of fudge.

"I did excellently over the weekend. I sold so many candles I was worried I wouldn't have any left in my shop. I put in a huge order for some more Saturday night though, and I might have to order even more before the day is done."

"That's what I like to hear. It makes me happy to see my friends doing well," I said and cut a slice of fudge for her and wrapped it up.

She nodded. "I'm pretty happy about it myself. Say, Mia, I heard about Hailey Strong. That she was murdered. Do you know anything about it? I suppose I shouldn't be asking, but you know how it is. In a small town like this, rumors start flying. I just can't get over the fact that she was killed and buried at the park like she was."

I put her piece of fudge into a decorated paper bag and folded over the top and set it on the counter. "I agree, it's awful. Ethan doesn't know much about it at this point."

She nodded and looked over her shoulder, then turned back to me. "Between the three of us, my sister works at the high school in the attendance office. She said Hailey was a real handful. She was in trouble all the time when she was there, and they worried she wouldn't be able to graduate. I don't know if that means anything, and maybe it's just idle talk, but it was the first thing I thought of when I heard she was dead."

"What kind of trouble did she get into?" I asked, lowering my voice even though we were alone in the shop.

"I don't know a lot about it. We had had this discussion last year when I asked her about students that might not graduate. I just had never thought about it before, and I wondered if they had many that might be in jeopardy of not graduating. My sister isn't supposed to be talking about students, so please don't let this get around, but apparently, Hailey was a troublemaker. Her parents had to come down to the high school several times because she fought with other girls and was always having boy trouble."

"Boy trouble?" Christy said.

I put my hands on the front counter. "Really. That's interesting to know."

She nodded. "I guess she shouldn't be talking about the students, but she's my sister, and occasionally we do. Not often of course, but when I heard who it was that was murdered, I just felt like maybe that was something Ethan needs to know about."

"I'll let him know and tell him that it needs to be kept quiet. He'll keep your secret." I picked up a white cloth to wipe down the top of the counter.

She nodded. "I hope they find her killer soon. It just makes me sick that a young woman was murdered. Do they know how she died yet?"

I shook my head. "No, Ethan's waiting on the report from the medical examiner."

She nodded and Christy rang up her fudge. "Well, with Ethan on the case, I feel safe. I just feel bad about Hailey."

"We feel bad about it too," Christy told her. "I just can't imagine what her family is going through. Her life was just starting, and now it's over."

She nodded and picked up the bag of fudge. "Well, I had better get back to the shop, otherwise we'll be late opening. Tell your mother I said hello and that I certainly appreciate her fudge."

"We sure will," I said as she left the shop.

Christy turned to look at me. "Girls who get into trouble at school sometimes get into real trouble later in life."

I chuckled and shook my head. "Thank goodness most seem to grow out of it by the time they get out of high school. But you're right, her murder might be a holdover from someone she had trouble with in high school."

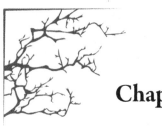

Chapter Eight

JOEY HARPER WASN'T hard to find. He worked at the Happy Feet shoe store. After Christy and I got off work the following day, we took a drive over there. If you looked at the weather outside, you would think it was a bit premature to be thinking about boots and sweaters, but sitting in the window was an array of suede and leather fall boots.

"Well, will you look at those," Christy said, looking into the window at a pair of rust-colored suede boots that came up past the knee. "Aren't they a pretty little pair?"

"Do those boots speak to you, Christy?" I asked. It was too hot to look at boots, but I had to admit, they were cute.

She nodded. "Oh yes. They're saying, take me home, Mama. And I'd hate to disappoint them."

I chuckled and pushed open the front door. The air conditioner was going full blast inside the shoe store, putting me in a slightly better frame of mind for looking at fall boots.

"Oh, look at these," I said, picking up a pair of suede oxfords. They were a dark chocolate brown and were as adorable as any shoes I had ever seen.

"I can't look now, I've got to try on a pair of these boots." She picked up the display boot and ran a hand over the suede. "They're so soft."

"I think I've got to try on a pair of these shoes." I picked up the display shoe. The laces were rolled string, and I liked the way they looked with the suede.

I glanced around the store. There was one other customer, and Joey Harper was waiting on them at the front register. I brought the shoe over to where Christy stood with the boot in hand.

"They're pricey," she whispered, turning the boot over.

"I figured they would be," I said. "Aren't these shoes cute?"

She looked at them now. "They really are cute. I wonder what other colors they come in?"

"I don't know, but at this point, I would buy a pair in every color. I wish fall would hurry up."

"You and me both." She set the boot back on the display and looked around the store. "They've got a lot of fall shoes and boots in already."

I nodded as she picked up a pair of suede tennis shoes in pink.

"That's cute," I said, coming to stand beside her.

"I don't have money to spend on shoes. Honestly, I need to pay rent and all those obnoxious things called bills. What am I going to do?" She glanced around at the shoes on display again.

"We might need to get a part-time job so we can buy all the shoes we want," I suggested.

"I know, right?"

The woman Joey was waiting on left the shop, and he turned in our direction and smiled, then came over to greet us.

"Hello, ladies. Is there something I can help you with?"

"We're just looking at all your new fall shoes and boots," I said. "You've got a lot of really cute things in."

He nodded. "We just got a shipment in last week. They sent us a lot of nice fall shoes, and we're starting to get our boots in too, as you can see. We'll get another big shipment in next week, too."

I glanced at him. Joey was tall, slightly over six feet I'd guess, and had a thin build. His blonde hair was a little on the long side. He wore a thin tie and a white button-down shirt and black pants.

"I can hardly wait," I said. "I love shoes, and don't get me started on the boots. I need at least one more pair of boots this fall. One of my old pairs wore out last year."

He nodded. "A girl can't have too many pairs of boots." He chuckled, but it sounded awkward.

"How have you been, Joey?" Christy asked him. "Haven't seen you around the candy store lately."

He nodded. "Yeah, I was thinking about stopping in to get some pumpkin spice fudge before it's gone again."

"You better hurry," I advised. "Joey, I heard your girlfriend, Hailey Strong died. We just wanted to stop by and tell you how sorry we were."

He frowned. "Thank you. I appreciate you thinking about me. I just can't believe she's gone."

Christy nodded. "I can't imagine how shocking that must have been when you were told. Do you have any idea what happened to her?"

He folded his arms in front of himself and his brow furrowed. "One day you're planning your next date and the next, she's gone. It's crazy and I can't get used to the idea of her being gone." He shook his head slowly. "I really don't know what happened to her. But to be honest, it doesn't surprise me that she ended up dead."

Her death might not have surprised him, but hearing him say that did surprise me. "What do you mean? I would imagine hearing that your girlfriend had been murdered would surprise a person."

He shook his head. "We've been together since the end of our junior year in high school. I thought I'd be with her forever, if you want to know the truth. But, for the last six or eight months, Hailey was running around with some different people. I didn't like it at all."

"What do you mean, different people?" I asked, picking up a smooth leather penny loafer. It was a reddish-brown and was as cute as anything else in the store.

"There were just some weird people that she like to hang around with is all. Ever since she started college last fall, it seemed like she changed. She wanted me to go to college too, and at first I thought I was going to, but then when I was offered a full-time position here at the shoe store, I decided that making money was more important than going to a junior college where all I'll ever be able to earn is an Associates Degree. What would I do with that?"

"You could've used it to go on to earn a bachelor's degree," Christy suggested. "A lot of people go to a junior college for the first two years and then transfer to a four-year school later. It saves a lot of money."

Joey half-rolled his eyes at the suggestion, but then caught himself. "Sure, I guess I could have done that. But I thought I would take a little time off from school and try to figure out what it was I wanted to do with my life. But Hailey, she was determined she was going to start school right after high school."

"I think that's a pretty logical step," I said, trying not to sound like I was inferring anything about what he had just said. Some people aren't cut out for college, and that was fine. There was nothing wrong with getting a job and working hard. But it sounded like Joey may have been a little jealous of Hailey moving on with her life.

He nodded. "Sure, I guess so. But then she started hanging out with these college people. She started drinking and going to parties. And there was one person in particular that I didn't like at all. Her professor, Frank Gillespie."

Her professor? "Frank Gillespie? What does he teach?" I asked.

"Literature. Can you believe it? He was reading her Shakespearean poetry." Now he did roll his eyes and smirked at the idea. "She thought it was so romantic."

"What do you mean by romantic? Was he making a pass at her?" I asked him.

His jaw twitched. "She wouldn't admit to anything, but she would sit around whining about how much she loved poetry and how much she enjoyed Gillespie's classes. I told her poetry was boring and that old guy sounded boring, too. I couldn't imagine sitting through a class like that." He snorted.

"So she was fond of his class?" I asked.

He nodded. "You better believe it. I had to listen to her talk about it every time we were together. She'd go on and on about what an awesome class he had, and why didn't I go to college and take his class." He shook his head. "No way. I couldn't sit through that class and listen to all that garbage."

"Lots of people like poetry," Christy said. "But I can see where if your girlfriend was talking about some other guy all the time, even if it was her professor, it could get irritating."

He turned to her. "Yeah, I just don't trust the guy. There was something about him that was all wrong. He had a party at his house for his students back in April, and Hailey insisted that we go. She made me dress up in a suit and tie. Can you believe it?" He snorted again. "But I went. Only because she bugged me about it for so long. And it was all a bunch of snooty people sitting around reading poetry. I was bored out of my mind."

"Did Gillespie pay special attention to Hailey while you were there?" I asked. I was beginning to get a picture of this professor, and I didn't like it.

His mouth made a straight line. "Yeah, he did. He kept coming around her and complimenting her on her dress. She was wearing a really short dress, and it was all the guy could talk about. It was ridiculous. After we left, I told her we were not going to any other parties like that again. I told her she needed to find a job and drop out of school."

I thought he was making a lot of assumptions by thinking he could tell his girlfriend to drop out of school and get a job, but I didn't say so. "Did he behave that way around any of the other girls?"

He shrugged. "I don't know. I guess I didn't notice. I was more concerned with Hailey." The bell over the door rang and an older couple walked into the shoe store. "Excuse me a minute." He walked over to the couple to see if he could help them.

I looked at Christy. "It sounds like she was enamored with her college professor."

"And I wonder if her college professor was just as enamored with her."

I nodded. "Wouldn't surprise me."

She set the boot she was holding back on the display. "Frank Gillespie and his wife used to live next door to me when John and I were first married."

I looked at her. "Really? Did he seem like a creep? Because the way Joey described him, it sounds like he might be."

She shrugged. "I didn't notice that about him, but he and his wife worked a lot. We didn't see much of them."

I put the shoe back onto the display. I had an idea that the college professor might be more interested in his students than he should have been.

Chapter Nine

WE LEFT THE SHOE STORE without buying a thing. If we waited another month, the fall boots and shoes would go on sale, and besides that, neither of us had money to throw away on shoes that we wouldn't even wear for at least another month or so.

"Where to next?" I asked, looking at her.

She shrugged. "I guess we can go get some pizza. Or, why don't we stop by Betty's Closet and see what they've got in for the fall?"

I looked at her. "Why? They won't run their sales for fall clothes for a while yet either."

"I know, but Hailey Strong used to work there. I don't know if she was still working there before she died, but she might have been."

"Oh, I see." I started my car, and we drove over to the clothing store.

When we walked through the doors of Betty's Closet, I glanced around. Like the shoe store, they had a lot of their fall clothing out already. There were lots of sweaters, coats, scarves, and knit hats. The place smelled like cinnamon and new clothes, and made me wish for fall.

"Oh, look at this," Christy said, heading over to a display of thick, chunky knit sweaters. They were folded up on shelves and came in a wide variety of colors. She picked up a pumpkin orange colored sweater and turned to look at me, holding it in front of herself. "Can't you just imagine this with a pair of chocolate brown suede boots?"

I ran my fingers over the sweater. It was a thick cable knit and would be warm and cozy for the coming cold weather. "It's adorable. I love the color." I turned over the price tag and inhaled. "But that's a not so adorable price. We really have to wait until the sales."

"I know, I just can't resist looking at things though. I swear, if I ever strike it rich, I'm not going to have a closet for my clothes. I'm going to have a separate bedroom. An entire bedroom. I'll put rows and rows of racks so I can hang everything, or display them on shelves."

I eyed her. "That sounds ambitious."

"You better believe it. Go big or go home." She picked up another sweater. It was hot pink, and she held it up in front of herself. "What do you think?"

"Hot pink goes well with your skin tone."

She nodded. "It does. I might have to get one of these, too."

I looked up as Betty Mays, the store owner, headed in our direction. She was wearing a silk dress in teal with black heels. No costume for her. I glanced down at my costume and then at Christy's costume. There was something about Betty Mays that made me feel like she looked down on the Halloween season. And maybe on us, too.

She smiled, her dark red lipstick penciled in perfectly. "Hello ladies, is there something I can help you with?"

"Oh, we just stopped in to take a look at what you might have for the fall. Summer has been fun, but we're more than ready for fall," I told her.

"I just wish the weather would cool off so I could wear sweaters," Christy added.

Betty looked us up and down and smiled again. "I'm with you on that. I love fall and winter. Actually, I just really love sweaters and boots and coats. How come warm weather clothes aren't as cute as fall weather clothes?"

I smiled. "I feel the same way about it. There's just something about cold weather clothing that makes me happy."

"What do you think about this sweater?" Christy asked, holding up the hot pink sweater again. "Do you think it looks good on me?"

She nodded. "It complements your skin tone. You should definitely get it."

"I told you it was perfect for your skin tone," I said.

Christy nodded and folded the sweater up carefully, put it back on the shelf, and turned back to Betty. "I'm absolutely going to come back and get it, but I have to wait until I get paid. And until there's a sale."

She nodded, tucking a lock of her short red hair back behind her ear. "I always wait for sales myself. There's no sense in spending money if you don't have to."

I nodded. "Betty, I heard about your employee, Hailey Strong. She still worked for you, didn't she?"

Betty folded her arms in front of herself and nodded. "Yes, she still worked here. Although between the three of us, I have to tell you if she hadn't died, she probably wouldn't have been working here much longer."

I wasn't sure if I was more surprised by what she said or the tone in which she'd said it. It was clear Betty didn't think much of Hailey.

"What do you mean by that?" I asked.

"The girl was lazy. I regretted the day I hired her. Of course, it took me a while to catch on to her, because when I was here at the store, she ran around like a little busy bee. But word from the other girls got back to me. She was lazy, and as soon as I walked out the door, she would slack off and the other girls would have to do her job for her." She rolled her eyes. "Some people."

"Oh, that's a shame," I said carefully. "I hate having to work with people like that."

She nodded. "We all do. But here I was paying her good money to hang around the store and do practically nothing. I tell you, I need to check the security cameras more often."

Christy nodded. "That would be one way to catch someone like that."

"Still, it's a shame that she died the way she did." I tilted my head, looking at her, hoping she had some information that might be helpful.

She nodded. "Yes, it is a shame. I certainly would never have wished anything bad on her. Does Ethan have any idea what happened?"

I shook my head. "No, it's kind of early yet. But he's investigating, and I know he will figure out what happened before we know it."

She ran the tip of her tongue along her lower lip as she thought. "Honestly, the girl just seemed to find trouble. It was like she was a magnet for it. The other girls always talked about the way she would run around with different men, and twice I had customers come in here screaming at her because she had been fooling around with their boyfriends. I should have gotten rid of her months ago."

I was stunned by this. "They came into the store and started yelling at her?"

"Yes, I was so embarrassed. I had a talk with her. A long one. But did it help? No. Honestly, I know what kind of family she comes from and I should have known better than to hire her, but stupid me. I did."

She knew what kind of family she came from? Betty Mays had a reputation for being a snob. And that statement certainly said it all.

"So do you know anything in particular? Something that might lead to finding out what happened with her? Do you know if either of those women that came in accusing her may have still been holding a grudge?" I ran my hand across a sweater on the display.

She shrugged. "No, I have no idea. Although, I have my eye on her boyfriend, Joey Harper. There's something about that boy that I don't like. I was in the shoe store about a month ago and he started smooth-talking me. I couldn't understand it, complimenting me on my clothes and the shoes I was wearing.

But in the end, he hit me up for a job. Can you believe it? Why would I hire a man to work in a woman's clothing store? I mean, I guess it wouldn't be terribly unusual, but I just can't see it. All that complimenting and all he wanted was a job." She rolled her eyes.

She seemed miffed about Joey being nice to her just so he could ask for a job. I couldn't imagine anybody not being nice to a potential employer. Had she read something else into it up until the point that he asked about the job? Odd.

"Was Hailey a full-time employee here?" Christy asked.

Betty snorted. "Goodness, no. I can't imagine having to put up with that girl for forty hours a week. She only worked about twenty hours a week. She went to college during the day and worked here in the afternoons and evenings."

"I suppose working part-time is the most a lot of college students work," I said.

She nodded. "Hailey thought she was a sly one, that girl. She pulled a prank on her best friend, Shayna Gates. Shayna used to work here, but left back in December. She regretted ever leaving my employ, of course. She had it too good here. But Hailey pretended that I was interested in hiring her back, and then when Shayna came and asked me about the job, and I told her I wasn't hiring. You should have seen the look on the girl's face. She comes from a needy family, you know, and I'm sure that the prospects of a job meant a lot to her. She never should have left to begin with. What I should have done was fired Hailey and given her hours to Shayna. Oh well. But, I suppose I can do that now can't I?"

"Wait, she told her best friend that you were going to hire her?" I asked.

"Apparently so. Hailey told Shayna all she needed to do was meet with me, and that I was going to hire her back based on her recommendation. Of course, that was all a lie." She shrugged and straightened up a blouse that was hanging on a nearby rack. "Oh well, some people are so gullible." She turned around and walked away without another word to us.

I turned to Christy. "I don't know about you, but I would be pretty angry about something like that."

I nodded. "Me too. She probably felt pretty foolish, and Betty wouldn't have tried to make her feel better about it, either."

"That's no lie."

It made me wonder how embarrassed Shayna had been about Hailey making her look foolish. Was she holding a grudge? And did she get even with her?

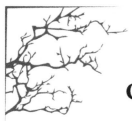

Chapter Ten

IT WAS FRIDAY NIGHT before Ethan and I got to spend any real time together. We decided to go out to dinner at a little steakhouse a few miles outside of town. It was the second weekend of Pumpkin Hollow Days, and tomorrow there would be a craft fair down at the park. The construction work had been finished, the hole filled in, and the barricade removed. It wasn't a moment too soon because once everyone heard about Hailey's murder, there were all sorts of lookie-loos hanging around, trying to get a glimpse of where she had been buried.

I looked over my menu and then closed it and laid it down on the corner of the table. "What are you going to have?"

He looked up from his menu. "I'm thinking about a nice juicy T-Bone steak. I love the steaks here."

"So do I," I said. "There's something about a charbroiled steak that I cannot pass up."

He nodded and laid his menu on top of mine. "I think I'm going to get the baked sweet potato and green salad with ranch to go with it."

"That sounds good," I said. "I may get the same thing." I picked up my glass of tea and took a sip. "So, what's going on with the case?"

He sighed, sitting back in his seat. "Poor Hailey may have been buried alive."

I gasped. "Are you serious?"

He nodded. "That needs to stay between the two of us."

"That's horrible. Who would do something that awful?" It made me sick to think about it.

His mouth made a straight line. "Horrible is right. I was stunned when I read the report. There was dirt in her nostrils, but it hadn't made it to her lungs. So the medical examiner isn't positive."

"But how? You said there wasn't any obvious trauma to her body. How did the killer get her to just lay there in that shallow grave?"

He sighed. "The medical examiner found traces of a sleeping medication in her bloodstream. Hopefully, she was completely unconscious when she was buried."

I groaned softly. "How awful. How could anybody be so horrible?"

He picked up his glass of iced tea and took a long drink, and then set the glass back down. "That's something I have never been able to understand, and I don't want to. I don't want to delve any deeper into the twisted mind of a killer than I have to. Just deep enough to figure out who did it and get them arrested."

I nodded. "I can understand that." Sometimes I felt sorry for Ethan. He was fairly sensitive, and I knew that some of these cases he worked on took a lot out of him. I hated it. But I knew that in other ways he enjoyed his job, and he was good at it.

"You know what I want to do tomorrow?"

I shook my head. "I don't know. What do you want to do?"

"Come over to the candy store and buy some pumpkin spice fudge, and maybe some caramel marshmallows, saltwater taffy, and just enjoy myself. For a few minutes, I'm going to pretend that I don't have anything better to do than to eat way too much sugar."

I grinned. "That sounds like a great plan. There's a craft fair at the park, maybe we can take a few minutes to take a walk through the park and look at the booths? You didn't get a chance to go to the vendors' fair."

He nodded. "That's a great idea. I do have to go to the station to do some work, but maybe we can go to the craft fair in the morning."

"That sounds like fun. Let's do it."

The waitress came, and we gave her our orders. When she left, he turned back to me. "So how are Pumpkin Hollow Days going? What are the other business owners saying about it?"

I nodded. "We've had a record turnout this year. I'm excited. This only the second year we've had Pumpkin Hollow Days of course, but we've had a bigger turnout than last year, and that makes me hopeful that this will be something that will continue for years to come."

"I'm sure it will be. People love coming here to take a look around and enjoy themselves. Even if it isn't fall or Halloween yet, it's still a lot of fun."

"Pumpkin Hollow is the best place to be. I'm glad we live here."

He nodded. "Me too."

"So have you gone for your tuxedo fitting yet?" I asked him.

His eyes widened. "I still have to do that. I have to make an appointment. I've been so busy that I haven't gotten around to it yet."

"I'll make the appointment for you, just give me an idea of a time that might be good for you."

He nodded. "I appreciate that. October is going to be here before we know it."

"It will be here so fast," I agreed. "I can hardly wait though. I've been looking at different floral arrangements, and we've talked to the florist. And, are you ready for this?"

"I don't know, am I?"

I nodded. "I have an appointment next week for a dress fitting."

He narrowed his eyes at me. "Wait a minute. Aren't wedding dresses supposed to be ordered like six months in advance?"

I sighed. "I'm surprised you know that. But, yes, you're supposed to buy a wedding dress at least six months in advance, especially if they have to alter it. But Amanda's mom is an excellent seamstress, and if I have any issues, she will take care of it. Besides, I don't want a really expensive, fancy dress. I just want something pretty and that I feel good in."

He studied me for a minute. "You're having second thoughts, aren't you?"

My eyes went wide. "Second thoughts? What are you talking about?"

He shrugged. "It seems like you're dragging your feet a little."

"Me? You're dragging your feet about the tux fitting. Are you having second thoughts?" I narrowed my eyes at him and leaned forward.

He chuckled and shook his head. "Never. Maybe we should have had a simpler, smaller wedding."

"I'm kind of thinking that that might have been a better idea. I mean, we're having the reception in my mom and dad's backyard. How fancy does my dress have to be?"

"Only as fancy as you want," he said.

We turned as a couple approached our table. It was Hailey Strong's parents. They looked tired and worn out.

"Hi Ethan," Jenny Strong said, and then she turned and nodded at me. "Hello, Mia."

"Hi, Jenny, Arnold. I'm so sorry about Hailey. It's just so awful."

There were dark circles beneath her mother's eyes. "It's unbelievable. I still can't get over it." She clutched her purse against her body. "Ethan, are you any closer to making an arrest?"

Ethan shook his head. "Not yet. But I promise you that we will find her killer as soon as possible."

She nodded. "There was something that we forgot to mention to you." She glanced at her husband and then turned back to Ethan. "A few weeks before Hailey died, she and her best friend, Shayna Gates, got into a fight. Hailey said she never wanted to see Shayna again. I couldn't understand it because the two had been friends since kindergarten. But she insisted she would never speak to her again."

"Did she say what the issue was?" Ethan asked.

"She wouldn't say what it was," her father said. "I don't understand it either. The girls had been friends forever. Sure, in junior high and high school they would occasionally have spats, but they usually patched it up within a few days. But this time, Hailey said she was done with her, and she hoped that she would die."

My eyes went wide. "Hailey said she hoped that Shayna would die?"

He nodded somberly. "I thought she was just being melodramatic. She couldn't mean anything by it. But it was something that was out of character for her. You know? She wasn't the sort of girl to say something like that."

I glanced at Ethan, his brow was furrowed.

Ethan nodded. "I'll certainly talk with Shayna and see if she can offer any insight into what happened to Hailey. Hailey didn't give you any hint at all as to what happened?"

They both shook their heads. "No, none at all. I asked her about it several times, and she would just get quiet and say she didn't want to talk about it," her mother said. She looked at her husband again. "Well, we don't want to disrupt your evening. We just wanted to let you know about this in case it's helpful to the investigation. Not that we really believe Shayna could have done something like murder Hailey. She's a nice girl."

Arnold Strong nodded. "It's just something that we remembered and thought maybe you should know about it."

"I appreciate you telling me," Ethan said. "You never know where something might lead."

They both nodded, and moved across the room to an empty table.

I looked at Ethan. "That's weird. I mean, I know Hailey was still young, and people her age can be dramatic, but saying she wished her best friend would die? And yet it was Hailey that ended up dead."

He nodded. "It was Hailey that ended up dead. I haven't had a chance to talk to Shayna yet, so I'll definitely be stopping by to talk to her."

"Makes me wonder what they argued about."

He nodded. "Makes me wonder, too. I'll find out and get to the bottom of it."

I didn't doubt that Ethan would find out who killed Hailey. What Betty Mays said about Hailey setting Shayna up and telling her she had helped her get her job back made me wonder. I could see where Shayna would be angry. But would she be angry enough to kill Hailey over it?

Chapter Eleven

I GRABBED ETHAN'S HAND when we got out of his truck. The craft fair was going to be a lot of fun. There had been a hum of excitement throughout the town when local crafters, as well as crafters from out of town, were invited to sell their wares. I hoped there would be a lot of fun Halloween themed items for sale so I could add to my growing collection.

I squeezed his hand. "I'm so glad you were able to take some time off so we could do this."

He grinned at me. "Me too. I told the chief I was going to take an hour or two and enjoy myself. I've already put in four hours at work this morning, so he didn't have a problem with it."

"I noticed you were gone early this morning. It's a shame you'll have to go back to the station, though."

He nodded. "I don't have a choice about it," he said as we walked up to a booth that sold wood crafted items. There was an adorable painted pumpkin sitting right in the middle of the booth table.

"How cute," I said, picking the pumpkin up and looking at it. The artist had put a lot of detail into the face.

"That is cute," Ethan said. "Look at that."

I looked up. He was pointing at a hand-painted wooden sign that said Pumpkin Hollow, land of Halloween. It was cute with pumpkin vine tendrils along the side and small jack-o'-lanterns painted on the corners.

"Oh, I really like that," I said, stepping closer.

"How are you folks today?" the woman working the booth asked us.

I smiled at her. "We're doing great. You have some really cute things here."

She nodded. "Thanks. I appreciate hearing that. I've been working on Halloween items since Easter." She chuckled. "My husband thought I was out of my mind, but I told him I was coming to the Pumpkin Hollow Days craft fair if it was the last thing I did."

"Well I for one, am glad that you did," I said. "Everything you have is so cute." The booth table was filled with a variety of painted wooden signs and pumpkins.

"Thank you kindly," she said. "If you want to know anything about any of my items, just ask."

"I will." I glanced back at Ethan. "I think I've got to have that sign. It would look cute hanging on my door."

He nodded. "Then you had better get it now. Somebody else will come along and snatch it right out from under you."

I looked at the woman. "I think I'm going to take that sign." I pointed at the one hanging up.

Ethan paid for the sign and we moved down the sidewalk with Ethan carrying the sign beneath his arm. I turned to him. "Thank you for buying the sign for me."

"Well, I look at it as I'm actually buying it for myself, too. Since we'll be married pretty soon."

"Then you came up with a good plan."

"I'm smart like that." He winked at me.

"Oh look," I said when I spotted some handmade candles in another booth. "I've got to check out the candles."

He followed me over to the candle table. "I don't doubt it."

"Hi folks," the man behind the booth said. "All our candles are handmade, with natural soy wax, and all-natural essential oils for scent."

I picked up a deep purple one in a pint-sized mason jar and inhaled. "Oh my gosh, plums." I held it up to Ethan, and he smelled it.

"That smells good."

"It does," I said, inhaling again.

The man looked at Ethan. "Glad you brought the wife by. She seems to love candles."

"That she does," Ethan said without correcting him. He winked at me when I glanced at him.

I looked over all the different colored candles and started picking them up and smelling them. They were heavenly.

I looked at Ethan. "I sure hate to go behind Polly's back and buy candles from somebody else."

Ethan chuckled. "We don't have to tell her, you know."

I nodded. "That's not a bad idea. I think I've got to have this plum candle." I picked up the purple one I had started with and the man wrapped it up and put it in a bag for me. I paid for the candle and we moved on down the sidewalk to look at more booths.

The sun was shining, but the day was going to be cooler than the past couple of weeks, and I was happy about that. I had the day off from the candy store, and I'd spent the morning cleaning my house and doing laundry. It felt good to not wear a costume today. I had braided my hair into two braids and wore an orange T-shirt and white shorts.

We wandered down the sidewalk that went through the middle of Pumpkin Hollow Park. There were just as many craft booths as there had been vendor's booths the weekend before. Getting to see everyone's wares was a lot of fun.

We stopped in front of a booth that sold small vintage and antique items, and I picked up a clear glass bottle with measurements on it. There was a mother cat and two kittens embossed on it.

"This is interesting."

"Do you know what that is?" the man behind the booth asked me.

I looked at him and shook my head. "No, what is it?"

"That is an antique baby bottle."

I looked at him in surprise. "Seriously? It's a baby bottle for a real baby?" It may have been a silly question, but the bottle was flat with measurements along the sides for every ounce up to eight ounces. I'd never seen anything like it.

He chuckled. "For real live human babies. It was used probably around the 1920s or 1930s."

"Wow," I said, looking it over. I held it up to Ethan so he could look at it.

He took it from me. "That is interesting," he said. He turned to me. "I bet you'd like to have it?"

I chuckled. "It's almost like you can read my mind. It would look cute on my fireplace mantle. I don't know what I'll do with it other than just sit it there, but I really like it."

He nodded and handed it to the man. "Go ahead and wrap it up and I'll pay for it."

I looked over the rest of the items in the booth and found a small tin toy that had Halloween decorations on it. "I think I have to have this too," I said to the man.

He nodded and wrapped it up in a piece of newspaper and slipped it into the bag that he had put the bottle into. "You bet. I tried to dig up all the Halloween themed items I had, but I didn't have nearly as much as I'd hoped for. I own a little antique shop over in Truckee. I was real happy to hear about this craft fair. It's fun to get out of the shop now and then."

I nodded. "I bet. I would think it would be a lot of fun to own an antique store."

"I've owned it for nearly forty years, and I can tell you it is a lot of fun. It's interesting seeing all the different things that come my way."

I looked at Ethan. "We need to open an antique shop here in Pumpkin Hollow."

Ethan shook his head and laughed. "We'll have to think about that."

We looked at the man's booth for a few more minutes and then we headed on. When we got to the end of the line of craft booths, we stopped and turned around. There were some vendors selling hotdogs, tri-tip sandwiches, nachos, and an assortment of fair food.

"I'm hungry," I said to Ethan.

He nodded. "I could use a bite, too. What are you thinking about getting?"

"The hotdogs smell amazing," I said turning to the hotdog booth. "I know we could have tri-tip sandwiches, but those hotdogs smell so good."

"Hotdogs it is," he said, and we went and got in line. We ordered onion rings and sodas to go with the hotdogs, and then took our plates and found a shady spot beneath a tree. We sat down on the grass, and I took a bite of my hot dog.

I nodded. "I'm so glad we got hotdogs. This is perfectly cooked and tastes so good."

He nodded. "You can say that again. There's just the right amount of charring on them."

"Nothing beats a slightly charred hotdog," I said and chuckled. My eyes went over to the playground where Hailey's body had been buried. They had placed a rubber surface all around and underneath the playground equipment that would absorb some of the shock from a fall. I sighed.

"I heard that sigh. I'll find her killer. It's the only thing I can do for her at this point."

I nodded and took another bite of my hot dog. And then something in the grass caught my eye. I swallowed and put my hot dog down on my plate, and leaned forward, picking up a white object. I held it up. "Look at that." It was a kid's white plastic barrette.

"Look at that," Ethan said in surprise. "I think I have the match to that."

I held it out to him. "Oh, I got fingerprints on it now."

He picked up a napkin and wrapped the barrette in it. "That's okay, we'll just discount your fingerprints when we send it to the lab to get prints off of it."

"What about the other barrette? Were there any fingerprints on it?"

He nodded. "Yes, but they were all smudged. I had hoped we could get one clear print off of it, but we couldn't."

"I hope I didn't ruin your chances of getting one off of that one. Do you think it belonged to Hailey?"

He shrugged. "It's a possibility. Or it could be anyone's."

"You don't see barrettes like that in the stores anymore," I said. Ethan hadn't shown me the other barrette, but he described it as being something that looked vintage, and he was right. It was in good condition, but it looked like it had been around for a while.

He nodded and took another bite of his hotdog. "Maybe we'll get a break with this barrette."

I looked over at the man with the antiques booth. "Can I see it?"

He gave it back to me, and I trotted over to the man's booth.

He smiled at me. "Did you come back for something else?"

I nodded. "I was hoping you could tell me something about this?" I unwrapped the barrette but left it laying on the napkin. "Does this look vintage to you?"

He leaned over, looking at it. "I believe those were popular in the 1960s or 70s. They aren't worth a lot, but they're fun to look at now. Why?"

I shrugged and wrapped it back up. "I just wondered. Thanks for the information."

I couldn't imagine why a pair of old barrettes would be near the murder scene of a young woman, but hopefully, this one would have some prints on it. I hoped Hailey Strong's murder would be solved soon so her family could get some closure.

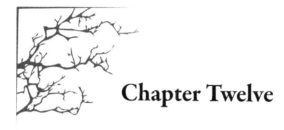

Chapter Twelve

"GUESS WHO MOVED INTO my apartment complex?" Christy asked me as we packed up candy orders to be mailed out.

I turned and looked at her, a roll of packing tape in one hand and scissors in the other. "Who?"

"Frank Gillespie."

My mouth dropped open. "*The* Frank Gillespie? The one that Joey Harper said might have been trying to hit on his girlfriend, Hailey?"

She smiled and nodded. "The one and only. I spotted him unloading a small U-Haul truck yesterday evening. I would have gone over there to talk to him, but I was afraid I'd get roped into helping him move heavy boxes into his apartment and there is no way I was going to do that."

I chuckled and sealed the box of pumpkin spice fudge I had just packed. "I wonder why he was moving into an apartment? I would think at his age he would have had his own house by now."

"He did. Remember, he used to live next door to John and me when we were first married. He and his wife made themselves scarce during the day so we didn't talk much, but we'd wave as we passed one another on the way in or out."

"That's interesting," I said thoughtfully. "What about his wife? Was she moving in, too? Or was it just him?"

"If his wife was with him, I didn't see her. She could have been at their old house packing things."

"Did he see you? I wonder if he would remember who you were?"

She shook her head. "No, I was peeking through the curtains so he didn't see me."

"Well, I think we need to have a little chat with him. I wonder if he has anything to say about Hailey's death. Or if he even knows."

She nodded and wrapped a gift tin of fudge with bubble wrap.

"It wouldn't surprise me if he has a lot to say about it. Not that he'd be saying it to us, of course. But I have a sneaking suspicion he might know something."

I thought my sister might be right. And I had to wonder if there might be trouble in paradise with his marriage. Maybe that was why he was moving into an apartment by himself.

When we had finished packing all the orders, we got to work in the front of the store straightening, dusting, and refilling shelves. Pumpkin Hollow Days was a smashing success so far, and I couldn't be happier.

When Christy and I finished our shift at the candy store, I drove her back to her apartment. I parked my car, and we walked slowly up the sidewalk, keeping an eye on Frank Gillespie's apartment. There was a car parked under the carport marked with his apartment number so he had to be home, but there was no one outside.

"Now what do we do?" Christy asked as we stood there and stared a hole through his apartment door.

I looked at her. "We need to bring him a welcome to the apartment complex gift. Got anything lying around your apartment we could give him?"

She narrowed her eyes at me for a moment and then brightened. "I just happen to have something."

We headed to her apartment, and she unlocked the door and let us in.

"What is it? You can't give him something used."

She chuckled. "It's not used. Not yet, anyway." She picked up a small gift tin from the candy store. "There was some leftover pumpkin spice fudge yesterday. I accidentally packed up a half-pound tin instead of a one-pound tin. I didn't have any more orders for a half-pound, so I brought it home. It got too late to snack on something this sweet late last night, so I never opened it up."

"Well, thank goodness. That's the perfect welcome gift," I said. "Let's go see how Mr. Gillespie is doing."

She nodded, and we headed back out the door and over to his apartment, and she knocked on his door. While we waited, she held up the tin and sniffed it. "I really hate to give this away."

"You can make more tomorrow. This one is needed right now."

She nodded, and the apartment door opened. Frank Gillespie looked at us, perplexed. "Can I help you?"

Christy grinned. "Hello, Frank. How are you doing today?"

Frank still looked puzzled. His eyes went to the tin in Christy's hand, then back to her face. "I'm fine. I'm sorry, do I know you?" He glanced at me.

Christy nodded. "Yes, we were neighbors six or seven years ago. Over on Autumn Avenue."

His eyes went wide as recognition dawned. "Of course. You are—I'm sorry your name escapes me. My memory isn't what it used to be."

"That's okay, I'm Christy Jordan, back then I was Christy Green. This is my sister, Mia Jordan. Our parents own the candy store over on Spooky Lane, and I noticed you moving in yesterday, so we decided to bring you a tin of pumpkin spice fudge. I hope you like pumpkin spice. And fudge."

His eyes went to the tin again, and he smiled. "Well, that's kind of you. I love the fudge at your candy store. I just don't get over there often enough to get some."

Christy handed the tin to him. "Our mother makes the best fudge in the world."

He nodded, looking the tin over. "Pumpkin spice, did you say?"

She nodded. "Yes, pumpkin spice. We only make it during Pumpkin Hollow Days and for fall, during the Halloween season."

"This is a nice apartment complex," I added. "I'm sure you'll be happy here."

He looked at me and smiled. "Yeah well, I'm afraid I came under not so happy circumstances. My wife and I split up." He shrugged. "This place will do until I figure out what I want to do with myself."

"I'm sorry to hear that," Christy said. "My husband and I got divorced, too."

He smiled now. "Oh? So you're single?"

I didn't like how he jumped to that question so quickly, and I sensed that Mr. Gillespie might have an eye for younger women.

Christy shook her head. "No, I've been seeing someone for quite some time now."

Frank looked disappointed. "Figures. The pretty ones are always taken." Then he looked at me. "How about you? You single?"

The question surprised me. I shook my head. "No, I'm getting married in a few months."

He frowned. "Oh. Figures."

Christy crossed her arms in front of herself. "So, are you still teaching at the college?"

He nodded. "Oh yeah. I'm sure I'll do that until I retire. It's a nice little school, and I always enjoy the kids."

"I bet it's a nice place to work," Christy said. "Did you hear what happened to one of the students there? Hailey Strong?"

He frowned again, and I watched him carefully. Was that a flicker of something I saw in his eyes?

He nodded. "It's a shame; she was a good girl. I had her in one of my classes last year. She was a good student, and I hated to hear what happened to her."

She was a good student? That made me wonder. According to Polly's sister, she was troublesome when she was in high school.

"I just can't imagine what could have happened to her," I said sadly.

He looked at me and nodded. "It seems crazy, doesn't it? I hope the police are taking a close look at her boyfriend."

"Joey Harper?" I asked.

He nodded. "He was so controlling of Hailey. Hailey complained about him from time to time. I told her a girl like her didn't need to waste her time on a relationship like that, and she should break up with him." He shrugged. "I don't know if she ever did."

"Did she say anything in particular about their relationship?" I asked him.

He looked at me a moment, then nodded. "Yeah, he accused her of cheating on him, and she swore up and down she never had. And I believe her. Like I said, she was a good girl, and I just can't imagine her doing that."

It bothered me that he kept referring to her as a girl. She was a young woman.

"I didn't know Hailey well," Christy said and glanced at me. "It's just sad that somebody so young was murdered. Her life just cut off the way it was."

He nodded and glanced back over his shoulder. "Say, would you girls like to come in? I could maybe order a couple of pizzas."

My eyes went wide. No way was I going into his apartment. There was something about him that I didn't like. "I'm sorry,

I've got to get home. We just wanted to stop by and say hello and welcome you to the apartment complex."

Christy nodded. "Yes, my boyfriend is coming over in a few minutes. Thanks for the offer though."

He nodded, looking disappointed. "Of course. Maybe another day."

Christy smiled but didn't agree to pizza with him on another day. I didn't either. There was something about this Frank Gillespie that bothered me. A lot.

"Well, thanks for the fudge."

We said our goodbyes and headed back to Christy's apartment.

"I don't like him," Christy whispered.

"Neither do I. You better keep an eye on him."

She nodded. "Believe me, I will."

I didn't know about Frank Gillespie. He put off a vibe that made me feel not so safe around him.

Chapter Thirteen

"I LOVE THE FUDGE YOU sell here," the woman in the princess costume standing in front of me said. She looked to be in her late fifties, but she wore the princess costume well.

"Thank you," I said nodding, and went back behind the front counter. "We love to hear that. Fudge is one of our specialties, and we all love to indulge in it as well as make and sell it."

She chuckled and peered into the display case. "Oh my goodness, you've got pumpkin spice fudge back?"

"We do. You had better get some of it because it's only here for another week or so, and then it won't be back until the Halloween season starts."

She nodded and looked at me. "I'll take a pound of it. It's my favorite. I'd also like half a pound of peanut butter fudge. I think that's my second favorite."

"I'll get that for you right now," I said, opening up the display case and removing the two trays of fudge.

She began humming as I got to work cutting the fudge and wrapping it for her. "Are you enjoying Pumpkin Hollow Days?"

She nodded. "I love it. I'm so glad that you all added this event to the summer months. But I'll be back during the Halloween season, too. Probably two or three times." She chuckled. "And that means return visits here to the candy store."

I smiled and put her fudge into paper bags. "We love hearing that, too. Return customers are our favorite kind of customers."

I rang up her fudge, and she paid for it and left the shop.

I turned and looked at my mom as she came out of the kitchen, her apron dotted with bits of fudge.

"It's getting hot back in that kitchen."

"You need a rest. You've been on your feet all morning long."

"You know what? I think I'm going to take a short walk and stop by Amanda's and pick up a coffee. Can I get you anything?" She untied her apron, folded it, and brought it over to me to put behind the counter.

"I would love a pumpkin spice latte. I can't get enough of it. Can you get it iced for me?"

"One iced pumpkin spice latte coming up. I'm going to go back to the kitchen and see if Linda and Christy want anything, and then I'm going to go for that walk."

"Take your time," I said. "We'll handle everything here."

She grinned and headed back to the kitchen.

I looked up as the front door opened, and a young woman walked through the door. She smiled at me and headed to the front counter.

"Hello," I said, turning to her. "Is there something I can help you with?"

She nodded, beaming. "Yes, I heard that you all might be hiring. Can I get an application?"

"Sure." I pulled out a printed form that my mother had made up and slid it across the counter to her. "I know my mother has hired several people, but I think she was still looking for one or two more."

She grinned. "That's great. I only need a part-time job, because I'm going to college in the fall. I don't think I could handle more than twenty or twenty-five hours a week."

I nodded. "That's a good number of hours that my mom can work with. She usually hires part-time help, and they usually work between twenty and thirty hours a week."

She held her hand out to shake mine. "Shayna Gates. Pleased to meet you."

I felt my eyes widen, and I hoped she didn't notice. "Mia Jordan. Pleased to meet you." I shook hands with her. "Oh, Shayna, do you have any experience in the candy-making business?"

She chuckled and shook her head. "Unfortunately, no. But I've worked at a diner, so I understand about handling food and being careful with it, and I used to work down at Betty's Closet."

Now was my chance. "Oh my gosh, did you hear that one of the employees at Betty's Closet died?"

Her eyes went wide now, and she nodded. "Yes, Hailey Strong. We were best friends." Her eyes teared up, and she looked away for a moment, then she turned back to me. "I just can't get over it. I can't imagine who would want to kill Hailey."

"I'm not sure that I knew Hailey," I said carefully. "But I can't imagine anybody murdering under any circumstance."

She nodded again. "What kind of crazy person would do something like that to her? I heard she was buried at the park. Who thinks of something like that? Why would they do that?"

I shook my head. "I wish I knew. So do you still work at Betty's Closet?"

She shook her head. "No, I quit last Christmas. Things were just crazy down there. I hate to speak badly of a former employer, but the owner there, Betty Mays, is really difficult to work for."

I thought she was probably telling the truth about Betty. There was something about her that suggested she was high maintenance, and I thought working for her probably wasn't a lot of fun.

"What do you mean by difficult?" I asked.

She shrugged and glanced at the display case. "You just couldn't make her happy. She was always complaining about everyone's work and sometimes she would encourage animosity between the employees." She looked at me. "Oh, sorry, I really shouldn't be saying these kinds of things. You're going to think I'm a terrible person and that I would be difficult to work with, but I swear I'm telling the truth."

"It's okay, some jobs aren't so great. I've had a few of them in my past. How did she encourage animosity between the employees?" This was interesting. I wondered if Betty Mays had caused problems between Hailey and Shayna.

She sighed. "She would tell one person that one of the other girls was complaining about her when she wasn't around. So, of course, that made them upset and they would go and confront the other girl, who of course, would say that she never said anything about her to begin with. We all finally got it worked out that Betty was just making things up at times. Not always, but sometimes."

"I wonder why she would do that?"

She shrugged. "I don't know. Honestly, Betty Mays is just a high maintenance person." She chuckled, but it sounded forced. "It seemed like she liked to stir up drama at work."

I nodded. "So was Hailey still working there before she died?"

She nodded. "Oh yes, she'd been working there for a couple of years." She glanced over her shoulder, but the candy store was empty besides the two of us. She turned back to me again. "Between the two of us, it wouldn't surprise me if Betty had something to do with her death."

Now we were getting somewhere. "Oh? Why do you say that?"

She shrugged again. "Maybe I shouldn't say something like that. But there's just something about Betty that I've never trusted. And she and Hailey had issues. You see, nobody knows about this except for me, but Hailey caught Betty cheating on her husband. And she held it over Betty's head." She frowned. "I told her she was going to regret doing that, but it didn't stop her."

I was shocked, to say the least. "How on earth did she catch her cheating on her husband?"

"She happened to run into her having dinner with some guy over in Truckee. I guess Betty thought she was safe since they were meeting out of town, but when she saw Hailey, she about fell over herself trying to come up with an excuse why she was there with this guy. Hailey said she probably wouldn't have thought much of it except for the way that Betty acted. She started getting nervous and claiming that it was her cousin. The guy looked at her like she was out of her mind when she said it, and Hailey put two and two together and accused her the following day."

"That's crazy," I said slowly. Maybe Hailey had died because she knew too much.

She nodded. "I told Hailey she was playing with fire and she needed to just drop the whole thing. I told her she should get another job someplace else because this wasn't going to end well."

"What did Hailey say to all of that?"

She sighed and her eyes teared up again. "She said she knew how to handle Betty Mays."

"That doesn't sound good."

She nodded. "You're telling me. It was a crazy situation. And now, I just have to wonder about what happened. I wonder if Betty got tired of Hailey holding her secret over her head and did something about it."

I was quiet a moment. "Maybe you should talk to the police about this."

Her eyes went wide again. "Oh no, I'm not getting involved in this thing. If Betty found out I went to them and told them, then I know she would come after me. That woman is crazy. I was never so happy to leave a job as I was when I left that one."

I nodded. "Well, I guess I can see your point." I wasn't sure she was telling the truth. If she was so afraid of Betty, why did she jump at the chance to work for her again?

There was no way I was going to keep this from Ethan. He needed to know about it. I didn't know whether it would lead anywhere, but it might.

Chapter Fourteen

THE FOLLOWING MORNING, I headed down to the Sweet Goblin Bakery for some donuts. I was working an early shift, and I knew everyone at the candy store would appreciate the donuts. I felt like I needed a donut in the morning these days, although it might not have been the best habit to get into.

I pushed open the bakery door and inhaled. "Something smells good today," I said to Angela.

She brightened when she saw me. "Good morning, Mia. I just pulled a batch of pumpkin spice muffins out of the oven."

"That must be what smells so good in here. I love the smell of pumpkin spice. I'm going to have to get some of those muffins." I went up to the front counter and looked into the display case. There were a dozen pumpkin muffins with streusel topping sprinkled over them in the front.

"They're what smells so good in here. I put cream cheese filling in the middle of them. Makes them extra special."

"Oh my gosh, for sure I am going to have to get some of those. I came for a dozen donuts, but I think I'm going to get half a dozen of your pumpkin spice muffins, and the rest donuts.

I hate to take so many of them, but I have an idea they are going to be very popular with everyone at the candy store."

"That's okay, I have two more dozen already made in the kitchen." She picked up a bakery box and unfolded it. "So Mia, how is the investigation going? I'm sure Ethan keeps you informed."

"Honestly, Angela, I know Ethan is doing all he can to find Hailey's killer, but I've barely had time to speak to him the last few days. We've been crazy busy at the candy store and he's working long hours on the investigation."

She nodded and opened the back of the display case. "I know, it's been crazy busy around here too. And I'm sure Ethan will catch her killer. I just can't stand the wait."

Before I could answer her, the bakery door opened and Ethan stepped through it. I smiled at him. "Were your ears burning? Angela and I were just talking about you."

He looked from me to Angela and back. "Oh? I hope you're saying good things about me."

"Of course we are," Angela said with a nod. "We were just discussing the investigation and how we both had confidence in you that you were going to find the killer."

"Well, I appreciate the vote of confidence," he said with a nod. He came over to me and gave me a quick kiss and turned back to her. "I'm doing everything I can to get her killer arrested as quickly as possible."

She stopped what she was doing, a pumpkin muffin in one hand, and looked at him. "You know what, Ethan? I've been thinking. What about her boss? I know Hailey had a lot of problems with that Betty Mays. They couldn't stand each other.

I told her I'd give her a job down here at the bakery if she wanted to quit her job, but she didn't want to work in food. She said she didn't want to go home smelling like donuts." She rolled her eyes and chuckled. "That kid. She was something else."

"Betty Mays," Ethan said thoughtfully and stepped up to the front counter. "Did she say anything specific about her that makes you think she might have had something to do with her death?"

"Well, between the three of us, Hailey caught her cheating on her husband. Ran into her with her boyfriend at a restaurant, and ever since then, Betty Mays was on her case. Hailey said Betty wanted to fire her, but she was afraid to because of what she knew. Hailey of course, would never have told anybody about the affair. She wasn't that sort of person. I mean, she wouldn't tell anybody except for her mother and me. But apparently, Betty was worried about her talking."

"Really? Did Hailey ever say that Betty threatened her in any way?" he asked.

"Yeah, one day she came in late to work and Betty said that some people were lucky they still had a job. And that some people were so nosy they didn't deserve to keep their jobs."

I crossed my arms in front of me. I hadn't had a chance to speak to Ethan about Shayna telling me the exact same thing. But Angela was wrong about Hailey. Shayna knew about the affair, so Hailey obviously didn't mind telling other people. It made me wonder how many people she told. Maybe it had gotten back to Betty that she was talking about the affair, and she got scared and killed her.

"It's definitely worth checking into," Ethan said, leaning against the counter.

Angela nodded. "I think you should." She turned to me. "What else did you want besides the muffins?"

"Go ahead and fill the box with whatever donuts you've got to make up a dozen. Everyone loves donuts, so it really doesn't matter which ones. Myself, I'm looking forward to that pumpkin spice muffin."

Angela nodded and got to work adding donuts to the box with the muffins in it. I turned and looked at Ethan. "What are you up to this morning?"

He grinned. "At the risk of looking like a walking cliché, I came to buy donuts for the station."

Angela chuckled. "Don't you worry about anybody making fun of you for eating donuts, Ethan. I eat plenty of them myself."

"I'm not worried. I'm going to eat donuts regardless of what anybody says," Ethan said, and wrapped his arm around me and gave me a one-armed hug. "I've missed you."

"I miss you too," I said, rubbing my nose against his arm. "We need to get together for dinner again. Soon."

He nodded. "We sure do. I'll try to get off at a decent time tonight or tomorrow night. Maybe we can go and get something then."

I laid my head against his arm. "That sounds great."

Angela finished filling the box of donuts for me and I paid for my order and waited, hanging around for Ethan to buy his. Angela filled three boxes with donuts for Ethan and after he paid for them, we stepped out onto the sidewalk.

"So what's going on with you?" he asked me, holding the three boxes in one hand.

"Not a lot. But Angela isn't the first person to tell me about Betty Mays and Hailey discovering that she was having an affair. Her friend Shayna came in to apply for a job at the candy store, and she told me the same thing. Makes me wonder if Hailey was telling a lot of people about it and it made Betty angry."

He nodded thoughtfully. "That's a possibility. No one would be too happy about someone exposing them if they were having an affair."

I filled him in on everything I found out of the past couple of days and I waited to see what he would say about it.

"I know Angela would like to believe that her niece was an angel, but there aren't many people besides her parents and her aunt that believe that. Sounds like she was running around sticking her nose into things that didn't concern her."

"I also think you should stop by and say hello to her college teacher, Frank Gillespie."

"He's already on my list," he said. "He was one of the last people who saw her alive."

I looked at him, one eyebrow raised. "Really? Who told you that?"

"I traced her last couple of days and she had gone to afternoon classes, and then got into her car and left the college. He taught her last class. She was taking summer classes to graduate early."

"It's funny that Frank Gillespie didn't mention she was taking a summer class with him at the college. He said he'd had her in a class last year."

"That's interesting. I guess I do need to have a talk with him."

"I think it's very interesting." I shifted the box of donuts in my hands. "I also wonder who had the keys to the heavy equipment at the park? How would they have been able to turn the equipment on and bury her without drawing attention?"

He looked at me in surprise and then smiled. "Didn't I tell you? They didn't."

"What do you mean?"

"The shallow hole was already dug. They were replacing the dirt around the playground with sand before adding that soft rubber covering over it that we saw Saturday. If the kids fall off the playground equipment, it will be a softer landing than hard dirt. But they realized they didn't have all the materials to finish the project, and they left the small shallow area they had dug up. The killer put Shayna in it and filled it in with the loose dirt from the hole, using a shovel."

"Well, that was convenient."

"It was a stroke of good luck. Or the killer planned it out after having seen the shallow hole."

"Interesting."

I didn't like the way Frank Gillespie made had made me feel when we talked to him and that made me suspicious that he might have had something to do with Hailey's death. But at this point Betty Mays seemed to have the best reason for killing her. If there was a possibility that Hailey might expose her affair, it might make her angry enough to kill her.

Chapter Fifteen

CHRISTY CALLED ME AFTER work the following day. I had just left her at work twenty minutes earlier, and she wanted me to come to her apartment immediately without explaining why. I hurried over, and as I walked across the apartment complex; I knew exactly why she called me. There was a big party going on over at Frank Gillespie's apartment.

I knocked on her door and she opened it almost before I was done knocking. "What took you so long?"

"I got in the car and came over as soon as you called me," I said, stepping into her apartment. "What's going on over there?"

She closed the door behind me and we moved over to her window. "Frank is throwing one heck of a party. I've seen young college-age kids going in there for the past hour." She pulled the curtain back, peering over at his apartment.

"You remind me of a little old lady hiding out in her apartment watching the party across the street," I said. "It's sad when you aren't invited to the party, isn't it?"

She looked at me, narrowing her eyes. "I do not want to go to that kind of party. It's crazy how loud the music is. I thought the parties from last month that were going on here were loud, but this is nuts."

"Do you recognize anybody that's gone in there?" I asked, looking through the window again.

She shook her head. "No, I don't recognize any of them. I certainly haven't seen his wife show up, either."

"Ex-wife," I corrected. "She probably had all she could take of his partying lifestyle and kicked him out."

"She did end up with the house, didn't she?" she said. "I wonder if this is going to go on all night?"

"It's summer, and they're all off on summer break. Probably so."

She shook her head. "I'm not going to listen to that all night long. What kind of music is that, anyway? It's horrible."

I chuckled. "I have no idea, but I can't imagine how you're going to get any sleep. Do you want to come to my house and spend the night?"

She shook her head. "No. Why should I leave my apartment when I happen to know someone in law enforcement that can break that party up?"

"Say no more." I chuckled again, and pulled my phone out of my pocket and dialed Ethan.

"Hey, Mia," he said answering the phone. "What are you up to?"

"I'm hanging out at Christy's apartment, and there's a wild party going on over here in the apartment across the way. Can you come and bust it up?"

He chuckled. "Is it creating a disturbance?"

"Oh, you better believe it's creating a disturbance. The music is horrible, and it's loud. Really loud."

"The only thing worse than horrible music, is loud horrible music. I'll be right over."

I put my phone back in my pocket and turned to Christy. "Your problems are about to be solved."

She nodded. "Good. I hate this apartment complex. I was so excited to move here because the apartments were so cute, but somebody's always throwing a wild party. The manager doesn't do anything about it, either."

"That stinks," I said, crossing my arms in front of myself and looking out the window again. "I wouldn't want to live here with all this going on."

"Hey," she said. "When you and Ethan get married, you're moving out of your house, right? Maybe I can rent it?"

I looked at her. "Ethan's moving into my house. Maybe you can rent Ethan's?"

She brightened. "It would be a lot of fun living across the street from you. You can make me dinner every night."

I laughed and shook my head. "No way. You're making us dinner."

"We'll see about that," she said and peered out the window as a young woman in a halter top arrived for the party.

TEN MINUTES LATER, Ethan arrived and stopped by Christy's apartment before going over to take care of business.

"I'm so glad you reported a wild party, Christy," he said, standing in her open doorway. "I didn't have anything else to do this evening." He glanced over his shoulder at the offending parties.

"No problem. They started up over an hour ago, and it's only gotten louder. You know who that is over there, don't you?"

He turned back to her and shook his head. "No, who?"

"Frank Gillespie. It seems he's in the habit of hosting parties for college students."

"Is he?" Ethan asked, looking at the party apartment again. "Well, I'm about to break this one up. You two stay here."

We watched as Ethan headed over to Frank's apartment.

"Maybe we should shut the door and hide?" I asked her.

"Why?" She looked at me, eyebrows raised.

I shrugged. "You called the cops and ruined his party. He might retaliate."

She shrugged. "I'm not afraid of him. I'm just annoyed because of all the noise. If he does retaliate, he's going to be sorry."

I grinned. "You know what? Why don't you give your notice to the apartment manager and come camp out in my living room until Ethan and I get married? We can put your stuff in storage and when we get Ethan's stuff moved out of his house, you can move in there. We'll put in a good word for you with the owner."

"I like the way you think," she said. "I might do just that. I can't tell you how much I'd appreciate getting out of here."

I nodded and watched as a young college girl answered Frank's door with a bottle of wine in her hand. Ethan flashed his badge at her and her eyes went big.

"Oh," Christy said as we watched. "Somebody's about to become very sad."

I laughed. "The cops are busting up the party."

"I wonder if that girl is old enough to drink alcohol?"

"That's a good question. She sure doesn't look like she is."

We watched as Frank made his way to the front door and Ethan talked with him for a few minutes. I could see Frank shaking his head. If I wasn't mistaken, his face was turning red. It was his own fault, thinking he could have a party that loud in this apartment complex and thinking no one was going to complain.

"He doesn't look very happy," Christy said as we stood at her open door and watched. Frank shot us a look and then looked back at Ethan.

"And now he knows who the perpetrators are," I said, leaning against the doorframe.

She snorted. "I'm not going to give him any more candy."

"Maybe you should pack a bag and come and stay with me tonight."

"I told you I wasn't afraid of him," she said, looking at me. "Are you?"

I shook my head. "No, but who needs the hassle?"

"Can't argue with you there."

The college students began filing out of Frank's apartment. "I wonder what the attraction is there? It's not like Frank is good looking."

"Well, I think the attraction is probably a passing grade," I said.

She looked at me and laughed. "Okay, maybe I do see the attraction now. Sort of. But summer classes are over, aren't they?"

"I don't know for sure. If they aren't out, I think they might be getting ready to take their finals just about now."

"Then I can see why they would come to a party at their teacher's house. Plus, free booze."

Ethan finished talking to Frank and walked back over to us. He was smiling. We stepped back into the apartment and he followed us and closed the door behind himself.

"Okay. Party handled."

"What did he say?" I asked.

"He was mad. Said he had a right to have a party in his own home. I told him that he could have a party in his apartment, but he couldn't disturb everybody else in the apartment complex. And I also said that some of his friends might be too young to drink."

Christy laughed. "What did he say to that?"

"He got angry and said they were all old enough to drink, and when I pointed out that I could ask for everyone's ID, he decided not to argue with me."

"Jerk," Christy said, looking through the window again.

"I had a great idea," I told him and kissed him. "Christy's going to move in with me until we get married, and then when you move in with me, she's going to move into your house. You can talk to the landlord about it, can't you?"

"That's a good idea," he said. "That way the landlord doesn't lose any rent money, and we can vouch for her so she'll be able to get in."

"And we'll get to do each other's hair every night just like when we were little," Christy said with a smirk. "Won't that be fun?"

I looked at her. "Actually, I do think it would be fun. You can practice wedding hairstyles on me."

"Well, my hair needs to be done pretty, too. You can also work on mine."

"It's going to be like having a sleepover every night, isn't it?" Ethan asked.

I nodded. "I think it will be fun. We haven't lived together since we were kids."

"And you can do all the cooking for me," she said.

I shook my head and turned to Ethan. "So what about that party, Ethan? All those college-age kids. There wasn't one of them over twenty-five, was there?"

He shook his head. "I really don't think so. Makes me wonder if Hailey attended many parties at his house."

"We know she attended at least one," I said. "Joey told us that."

He nodded. "It certainly isn't normal behavior. A man that age inviting all those young kids over for parties. I'll have another talk with him once he settles down from having his party disrupted."

I thought that was probably a good idea. Maybe he wanted more than a party with Hailey, and he got angry when she refused. "Do you have to go back to work?"

"I do have to get back to the station."

"That's a shame. I think Christy and I are going to get a pizza, and maybe we'll even pack a few things tonight."

Ethan kissed me. "Don't make me sad. I really could use some pizza."

"Maybe we'll save you some," Christy said.

"Deal."

Ethan kissed me again and left. I didn't like Frank Gillespie. There was something about him that I didn't trust.

Chapter Sixteen

I OPENED UP THE DOOR to the Little Coffee Shop Horrors and inhaled the scent of freshly ground coffee beans. Brian was behind the counter, and I spotted Amanda sitting at a table in the corner with their baby, Isabella.

"Oh goodness," I said and hurried over to Amanda's table. "You brought her!"

Amanda grinned. "I sure did. I told Brian she needed to come down and scope out the lay of the land. Someday this will all be hers, and she needs to get used to the smell of coffee beans early."

"I want to hold that baby," Christy said as she went to the counter and gave Brian her order.

"Of course you can hold her," Amanda said.

"She can hold her when I'm done," I told her and held my hands out for the baby.

Amanda handed her to me and I held her up against my chest and kissed her on top of the head. She had silky, fuzzy blonde hair and sparkly blue eyes. She smiled at me and wiggled.

"I think she likes her Auntie Mia," Amanda said.

"Of course she does," I said, pulling a chair out and sitting down, holding Isabella in my lap. "She's such a pretty baby. I could just hold her all day."

Amanda chuckled. "You can come over and hold her all day long if you want to. It'll give me a rest."

"I might take you up on that offer," I said. I turned to look behind me. "Brian, can you make me a pumpkin spice latte, please?"

He nodded. "Sure thing."

I turned to Amanda. "How are things going, Amanda? I feel like I haven't talked to you in forever. I haven't called because I'm afraid I'll wake up the baby."

She waved a hand at me, dismissing the idea. "Nonsense. Call me whenever you want to. She's got to get used to the fact that it's not going to be silent every time she sleeps."

"How is she sleeping?"

She sighed. "Well, she's getting better at it, but she's still waking up every four hours. That's up from every two hours, so it's progress. I can't wait until she sleeps all the way through the night."

"I bet," I said. "That has to be the hardest thing about having a newborn. No sleep."

"That and changing diapers. Between you and me, it's not my favorite thing to do."

I chuckled. "I don't think it's something anyone enjoys. So how have you been? I mean you, not the baby." I looked at her, one eyebrow arched. There were dark circles beneath her eyes.

She smiled. "I'm doing all right. I was a little worried about the hormonal stuff after having the baby, but it hasn't been too terrible. If this is as bad as it gets, I'll be fine."

"I'm glad to hear it." Isabella made a gurgling sound, and I looked down at her. "How about you, Princess? How are you doing?"

Amanda sighed. "I think she's doing all right. She's a fairly happy baby, and I can't tell you how relieved I am about that."

I leaned back in the chair and turned so I could see Christy and Brian. "You're not going to get to hold the baby today, Christy. I'm the only one who gets to hold her."

"You want to bet?" Christy asked as she paid for the coffees.

I chuckled and ran my chin over the baby's head. Her hair was soft, and she smelled good.

"I can't wait for you and Ethan to get married and have one of your own," Amanda said and took a sip of her iced coffee.

"I think you're going to have to wait a while. I really don't think I want to try to have a baby until we've been married at least a year or two. I want to just enjoy married life for a while."

She nodded. "I think that's a good idea. We didn't intend to have a baby so soon after we got married, but I wouldn't have it any other way now."

"Of course you wouldn't, this little girl is the cutest thing ever."

When Brian finished making the coffees, Christy brought them over and set the pumpkin spice latte in front of me, and then set hers down in front of the chair next to mine. "Okay, now share that baby."

Reluctantly, I handed the baby to her. "You're so greedy."

She sat down with the baby and inhaled the scent of her hair. "I don't care. Call me whatever you want to, as long as I get to hold this little girl. She's so sweet."

"What about you, Christy? How are you and Devon doing? Are we going to be hearing wedding bells for the two of you soon?" Amanda asked.

Christy's eyes went wide, and she shook her head. "No. Not any time soon. But that doesn't mean that we aren't doing well, because we are as happy as can be."

"Good, I'm glad to hear that." Amanda turned to me. "I heard about Hailey Strong. What a shame. Does Ethan have any ideas who did it yet?"

"If he does, he's not sharing it with me. I hope he finds the killer soon."

We turned as the front door opened and Amanda's mother, Connie Krigbaum walked in. "Oh, there's my granddaughter," she said and went over to the front counter to order a coffee. "I've got to hold her."

"Your granddaughter? What about your daughter?" Amanda said.

Connie chuckled. "And there's my daughter. How are you girls doing today? All of you?"

"We're doing great," Christy said. "I've got a cute baby to hold, so life couldn't be sweeter."

"I hear you," Connie said. When Brian made her coffee, she came and joined us at the table, setting her coffee down. "Christy, I hate to do this to you, but can I hold my granddaughter? I don't get to see her enough."

"I guess so," Christy said reluctantly, and handed the baby over to her. "But I want her back."

Amanda picked up her coffee. "What do you mean you don't get to see her enough? You're at my house practically every night." She took a sip.

"And the time when I'm not there holding this cutie just drags on and on. Honestly, I can't wait until she's old enough to have sleepovers at my house." She kissed Isabella on top of the head.

"If you had a crib or a pack and play at your house, she could come over very soon."

Connie's eyebrows went up. "Really? Are you certain you're ready to have her stay away from you overnight?"

Amanda thought about it. "Okay, maybe I'm not. I don't know what I was thinking. I doubt I could get through the night without her."

Connie nodded. "I told your father we needed to buy a crib to keep at the house. Maybe we can start with her coming over for a few hours on the weekend, and work up to having sleepovers when she's a little older."

"That's a great idea," Amanda said and took another sip of her coffee.

Connie turned to look at me. "All right, you know I'm going to ask, don't you?"

I nodded. "Yes, and no, as far as I know, Ethan hasn't found Hailey Strong's killer yet."

She nodded and lightly bounced the baby in her lap. "You know, several months ago I stopped in at Betty's Closet and the owner, Betty Mays, was there. She was talking to one of the other girls, and they were talking about Hailey, saying unkind things about her and complaining about what kind of employee she was."

"What did she say?" I asked, sitting up.

She shrugged and thought about it for a minute. "They said she was lazy. Betty said she was sorry that she ever hired her, and that when she got a chance she was going to rectify that situation."

"But she was still working there when she died," Christy pointed out.

Connie nodded. "But when they saw me, they started whispering to each other. I didn't hear a lot, but I did hear Betty say that one day Hailey would get what she deserved."

"Really?" I said slowly. "But you couldn't hear what she said as far as what that comment was about?"

Connie shook her head. "No. But it was incredibly unprofessional, and I was shocked that she said it where she could be overheard. That Betty Mays, I've never liked her. She thinks she's better than everyone else, and she gossips all the time. I wouldn't trust her as far as I could throw her."

I wasn't a fan of Betty's either, but even if she was mean and unprofessional, did that mean that she might kill Hailey? If it was true that Hailey had caught her cheating on her husband, that might be reason enough for her to kill. Especially if Hailey was holding it over her head and threatening to let her husband know about it. But I wasn't sure if she was capable of murder.

Chapter Seventeen

I LOOKED UP AS THE bell over the candy store door rang and Shayna Gates walked through the door. I smiled. "Good morning, Shayna, how are you?"

She was grinning and wearing a Rainbow Brite costume. She was wearing a blond wig with her costume, and came up to the counter. "I'm doing fantastic, Mia. Can you believe it? I'm so excited."

I looked at her, shaking my head slowly. "Can I believe what?"

"I get to work here. At the Pumpkin Hollow Candy Store. It's like a dream come true," she said and laughed. "When I was a little girl, I used to think how cool it would be to work here every single day and be able to eat all the candy I wanted."

I looked at her, my eyes going wide. "Work here?"

She nodded and her wig slipped. She pushed it back into place with one hand. "Yes, but I promise not to eat all the candy I want. There wouldn't be anything left to sell to the customers." She giggled.

I staring at her, taking this in. "Wait, you're working here?"

The smile slipped from her face. "Yes. Your mother hired me. She didn't tell you?"

I shook my head slowly and Mom stepped out from the kitchen.

"Oh, there you are, Shayna," Mom said, walking up to us. She turned to look at me. "Mia, I hired Shayna to work part-time here at the candy store. With all the orders we've been getting these last few weeks, I thought we needed another part-time employee. And look at her, isn't she adorable in her Rainbow Brite costume?"

I looked at Shayna and nodded slowly. "Yes, she certainly is adorable."

Christy came out from the backroom and looked at the three of us. "What's going on around here? Are you all having fun and I wasn't invited?"

I looked at her. "Mom hired Shayna to work part-time. Isn't that awesome?"

Christy's brow furrowed, and she looked at Shayna. "That's great. We can always use more help around here." She looked at me.

I nodded. "Well, what should we get started with, Mom?"

"Why don't you show her around the candy store? And then maybe she can help you start filling the shelves. Later we'll have her pack up some orders for us." She turned to Shayna. "I just know you're going to enjoy working here, and we are delighted to have you."

Shayna beamed. "Thank you, Ann. I'm just so excited to be here."

"If you'll excuse me, I've got fudge to make." Mom turned and headed back to the kitchen.

I looked at Shayna and then at Christy, and then back to Shayna again. "Well, Shayna, this is the candy store," I said and chuckled.

Shayna laughed and nodded, and her wig slipped down again over her forehead. "Oh, this thing. I should have put some bobby pins in it to hold it on straight. That's what I get for buying a cheap wig."

"Wigs are always a problem for me. Why don't we take a look around the store," I said and came out from behind the front counter. "We'll start back in the breakroom so you know where to go when you want to take a break."

I led her back and showed her where to stow her belongings in a small locker along one wall. Then I showed her the bathroom, and we headed back to the sales floor.

"Do you ever get tired of eating candy?" she asked as she followed me down the hallway.

I shook my head and looked over my shoulder. "Never. You would think we would get sick of it, but Mom is always making different recipes for different types of candies, and they're always wonderful, so we've got to try them out."

"I don't know how I'm going to keep myself from eating too much candy," she said.

When we headed back onto the sales floor, Christy was sitting on a stool behind the counter. "Don't forget to show her the kitchen and the area where we pack the candy to ship."

"We're headed there now," I said, and led the way into the kitchen. "And this is the kitchen where all the wonderful deliciousness takes place. And over in that corner is our packing and shipping department. After we pack up the candy, we put the packages on the shelves until the mailman comes and picks them up every morning."

She looked around the kitchen and the packing area and then turned to Mom. "Do I ever get to make candy?"

Mom shrugged, looking up from the pot she was stirring on the stove. "If you want to make candy, after you've been here for a little while, I might be able to train you on that."

She grinned. "I would love to know how to make the candy. It's always so good here."

Mom smiled and nodded. "We'll see about it after you've gotten a few weeks working here under your belt. It's going to be so busy around here we'll have to wait until there's a break in the business. Usually, between Pumpkin Hollow Days and the Halloween season we get a couple of weeks were things are a little slower."

I turned to Shayna. "Well, why don't we go back out front and we'll start dusting shelves and making sure all the candy displays are filled."

"I'm right behind you," she said as we headed back out front.

Christy was still sitting behind the counter. She held up a duster when she saw Shayna. "Here's a duster, you can start on the shelves. There's really never any dust because we like to dust every day so everything is kept neat and clean."

She nodded as Christy handed her the duster and her wig slipped forward again. "I don't think this wig is going to work out," she said and pulled it off her head. "Can I put it back behind the counter?" She smoothed her brown hair down with one hand.

I nodded and then caught sight of two little yellow barrettes in her hair. My heart started pounding. They looked similar to the white ones Ethan and I had found at the park. One near Hailey's body, and the other beneath the tree when we had lunch. Except that instead of a white poodle, these had a yellow duck on them.

"Those are cute barrettes you have in your hair," I said. Christy swung around to look at her as she tucked the wig beneath the counter.

Shayna's hand went up to one of the barrettes and she patted her hair again. "Thanks. They are entirely too young for me, but for some reason, they appealed to me, so I wore them today."

"Those are interesting," Christy said slowly. "I've never seen anything like that in the stores."

She looked at her and shook her head. "No, I think they're vintage. Aren't they the cutest? Now, should I just start on any of the shelves?" she asked, indicating the shelf that held glass canisters of gumballs, taffy, licorice, and other assorted pre-wrapped candies.

I stared at the barrettes in her hair. They looked like they belonged to a set. And it wouldn't surprise me if that set also included a pair of white plastic barrettes with a poodle on them.

When I didn't say anything, Christy spoke up. "Yeah, that would be great. You can start with those."

She went over to the shelves and I looked at Christy. Christy stared at me wide-eyed.

I turned back to Shayna. "You know what's interesting, Shayna?"

She turned and looked at me over her shoulder. "No, what's interesting?"

"What's interesting is that when Hailey's body was found, there was a small white plastic poodle barrette that looks like it probably goes to the same set that those duck barrettes you're wearing go to. Do you have white poodles in the set that you bought?"

Shayna sobered. "I didn't buy a set. I just have these two."

"Where did you get them from?" I asked, folding my arms in front of myself and moving closer to her.

She licked her lips. "They were given to me. They were a gift."

"Who gave them to you?" I asked.

She frowned. "Why? What difference does it make?"

Christy came out from behind the counter and stood beside me.

"Because a murder victim ended up with a very similar pair of barrettes near her body," Christy said. "That's why she's asking."

Shayna's eyes went wide. "I didn't kill Hailey. Is that what you think?"

"Didn't you?" I asked. "Maybe you were angry at her for setting you up and making you look foolish about that fake job offer at Betty Mays' dress shop. And maybe you took it out on her."

Her eyes got bigger. "How do you know about that?"

I shrugged. "Things get around town. I wouldn't blame you for being angry at her. But I would blame you for murdering her."

She shook her head and turned toward me fully. "I swear. I never touched Hailey. I wouldn't do something like that. Sure, I was mad. Hailey was always doing stupid stuff like that, and I guess I should have known better than to fall for it. I was angry, and I told her I was done with her a few weeks before she died. I decided I had just had enough, but I never touched her."

She looked sincere when she said it, but I was suspicious. "Where did you get the barrettes from?"

She swallowed. "Joey Harper. He gave them to me. I knew he had given Hailey the white pair, so I almost didn't take them from him, but in the end, I did. I don't know why."

"You're dating Hailey's boyfriend?" Christy asked incredulously.

She shook her head. "No. I'm not dating him. He did ask me out, but I told him I would think about it. And then he gave me the barrettes. He said he got them from an online auction site. They're vintage from the 1970s. I know they're for little girls, but there's something sweet about them, and I admired the ones that Hailey had."

"So the white ones really did belong to Hailey?" I asked. We had made the assumption, but we didn't know for sure.

She nodded. "Yes. She had a pair of white ones with poodles, and a pair of blue ones with cats."

I glanced at Christy. "I think I want to go get a coffee now." I turned back to Shayna. "Go ahead and keep dusting the shelves, Shayna. I'll let Mom know we're going to go get a coffee."

Shayna nodded slowly and turned back to the shelf and started dusting it. I went to tell my mother that we were going to step out for a few minutes so that Linda could come up front and wait on customers.

Chapter Eighteen

"WHERE ARE WE GOING?" Christy asked as we walked down the sidewalk.

"The shoe store," I said.

"Joey Harper killed Hailey?"

I nodded. "Looks to me like he did."

I pulled my phone from my pocket and called Ethan. The phone rang and eventually went to voicemail. I hung up and stuck my phone back in my pocket.

"No answer?" she asked as we walked quickly down the sidewalk. She was dressed as Dora the Explorer and I was dressed as Minnie Mouse. In any other town, we would have looked ridiculous, but this was Pumpkin Hollow and we fit in perfectly.

"No answer," I confirmed. "Maybe he's in a meeting or something." I was starting to breathe a little harder. We were walking as fast as we could without breaking into a run.

"What are we going to do?"

I shook my head. "I don't know. But the shoe store is open right now. There'll be other people there. Maybe we can just ask

127

him a few questions and see what happens, and then give Ethan a call later."

She nodded. "Yeah, it's a public place, so it's not like he could do anything if we did accuse him of murder."

I glanced at her and chuckled. "We aren't going to accuse him of murder. We can't do that." I knew better than to do that sort of thing, and the reason I knew better was that I'd done it a couple of times. Ethan didn't appreciate it, and I told him I wouldn't do it again. But we had just asked Shayna some pointed questions and had almost come out and accused her of it minutes ago.

"We really need to get to the gym," Christy panted.

I chuckled. "The gym? Why do you say that?"

She shrugged. "Because we've only walked three blocks and we're out of breath."

"Speak for yourself. I am breathing perfectly normally."

"Oh, the lies we tell ourselves. You hate exercise as much as I do, but one of these days a killer might chase after us and we will appreciate having gone to the gym. If we don't go to the gym, we will really, really regret it someday."

I glanced at her. My sister was over-thinking things.

"Dump the backpack. It will make the load lighter."

"I can't dump the backpack. It's part of my costume."

The shoe store was nine blocks away from the candy store, and by the time we got there, I regretted not getting in my car and driving us over. What were we thinking?

We paused at the door to catch our breath. Christy laughed at me. "So, you're breathing normally, are you?"

I narrowed my eyes at her. "All right, maybe you have a point about the gym. But we don't have to go to the gym. We can just get out and do some walking around Pumpkin Hollow. As soon as fall gets here. I like being outdoors anyway during the fall with all the leaves turning colors."

She nodded. "Sounds like a plan then."

I pushed open the door and inhaled the scent of leather. There were two other customers in the store and we went over to the boot display to wait until they left.

"Still no sale," Christy said and picked up the rust-colored suede boots she had looked at the other day. "I need these boots."

"I'd like to have a couple of new pairs of shoes and boots," I said, picking up a black suede pair of boots. They went to mid-calf and folded over and were a little slouchy.

"You've got a wedding to pay for, you can't afford new boots," she said. "But I don't have a wedding to pay for."

I looked at her. She was making sense now, and I didn't appreciate it. "I know, no new boots until the wedding is over and done with. But you have a bridesmaid dress to pay for and new shoes for the wedding, so it's not like you can just splurge on new boots."

She shrugged and put the boot back. "Fine. Be a killjoy."

"Have you gotten many of your things packed up? And did you give notice at your apartment?"

She nodded. "I gave notice and I've got nine boxes packed. It always surprises me how many boxes it takes to pack my belongings. I swear that I don't have much stuff, but then the truth is told once everything goes into boxes."

"You can say that again. Are you going to get a storage shed to put it in until Ethan moves out of his little house?"

She looked at me, a black suede oxford in her hand. "No, I think I'm going to store everything in Mom and Dad's garage. I don't think they'll mind."

I chuckled. "You don't think they'll mind."

When Joey had finished waiting on his customers, he smiled at us and came over. "Hello, ladies," he said with a nod. "Are you having second thoughts about buying those boots?"

I turned and smiled at him. "We would love to buy new shoes and boots. Actually, I'd love to buy several pairs of each, but I've got a wedding to pay for and she's got a bridesmaid dress to pay for. We're still waiting on the sale."

"When will these boots go on sale?" Christy asked, indicating the rust suede boots.

He shrugged. "We don't know very far ahead of time when the sales are going to run. About a week before the sale starts, they'll let us know. I haven't heard anything about those. Would you like me to get a pair of them in your size from the back so you can try them on?"

Christy looked at me, grinning. "Why yes, why don't you get them for me? I wear a size 6 1/2."

He nodded and headed to the back room.

I narrowed my eyes at her. "What are you doing?"

She shrugged. "I want to see if they feel good. If they don't, there's no use pining over them."

She had a point. But I knew better than to try on any of the shoes. No way could I resist once I had them on my feet.

Joey was back in a minute with the boots. We went over to the chairs and sat down, and Christy removed her shoes.

He pulled the stuffing from the boots. "Here you go, try these on," he said, handing her the box.

Christy slipped one of the boots on easily. "This feels wonderful." Then she slipped on the other boot and stood up. "They feel really good. More comfortable than I had imagined."

"We've had a lot of compliments on these boots," he said. "They're going to be very popular for fall."

I eyed him. "Joey, how are you doing? You've been on my mind. I know losing Hailey had to be a terrible loss for you."

He turned to me and frowned. "I still can't get over it. She's gone. I keep thinking I'm going to pick up the phone and call her, but then I remember she's not here anymore."

"It has to be incredibly hard," Christy said, walking in a small circle near where I was still seated.

He nodded. "I never thought I would have to live through something like this. When you're young, you don't think about things like that."

"That's the truth," I said sympathetically. But how broken up was he? He had already asked another girl out and given her similar barrettes to the ones he had given his deceased girlfriend. "You know what was odd?"

He looked at me and shook his head. "What's odd?"

"When Hailey's body was found, there was this cute little white plastic barrette found nearby. And then the matching barrette was found a week later. At first, we thought they probably belonged to a child who played on the playground, but then we realize that these were vintage barrettes and most kids today wouldn't be wearing a pair like that. Isn't that odd?"

He stared at me and swallowed. "Vintage barrettes?"

I nodded. "And then what's even odder, is Hailey's best friend, Shayna Gates, came to work for us at the candy store today and she was wearing a similar pair. But hers were yellow ducks, and Hailey's were white poodles. They look like they probably belonged to the same set."

He swallowed again and went pale. "I gave those barrettes to Hailey. I thought they were cute when I saw them on an auction site. And I gave a pair to Shayna, too." He shrugged. "Hailey always liked vintage things, and I intended to give the yellow ones to her, but she died before they came in the mail. What else was I going to do with them?"

"You gave your girlfriend's barrettes to another girl? Her best friend?" Christy asked. "And then you asked her out?"

He nodded. "Yeah, I guess I did. Like I said, what else was I going to do with them. Shayna's just a friend. It wasn't a date date. Just dinner." He shrugged again.

"Did you also kill your girlfriend?" Christy asked. "Did you kill her so you could be with her best friend?"

I stared at Christy, but she ignored me.

"Are you out of your mind? I would never kill her." His hands clenched into fists and his eyes went wide. "You know who killed her? It was Betty Mays. She couldn't stand Hailey. I told Hailey to quit her job and stay away from her, but she wouldn't do it. Or maybe it was her college professor. That guy is creepy. I don't know who did it, but I know I didn't."

"Why should we believe you?" Christy asked.

"I guess you don't have to believe me, but just because we argued once in a while doesn't mean that I would kill her. Why would I? I don't have a reason to kill her."

"Because you thought she was fooling around with her professor," I reminded him. "And he's some old guy, and it hurt your pride to know she was doing that."

His eyes went big, and he shook his head. "Look, I don't really know that she was ever fooling around with her college professor. I just wanted her to stay away from him because he's creepy. Those parties he had were creepy, too. But I never accused her of having an affair with him, and to my knowledge, she didn't."

I sat back in my chair, taking this in. Had we jumped to conclusions when he talked about Frank Gillespie? I'd been sure that he thought Hailey was having an affair with him.

He crossed his arms in front of himself. "Look, the only killer in this town is Betty Mays. She called Hailey and asked her to meet her at the park to look at their booth for the Vendors' fair Thursday evening. Hailey was annoyed because it was her day off, but she went anyway. I worked late, and I didn't expect to see her until the next day, but she never called me."

"You really think Betty did it?" I asked, feeling a bit deflated. A minute ago I had been certain he had killed Hailey.

He shrugged. "Or maybe it was her college professor, like I said. Maybe he was hitting on her, and she refused him, and he killed her. I told that to the detective. He's your boyfriend, isn't he?"

I nodded. "Yes, he is."

"Well, I was here at work the night she died. You can ask my boss. Not that it's any of your business."

I glanced at Christy. We'd forgotten to ask if he had an alibi or not.

Christy sat down in the chair and removed the boots, and put her shoes back on. "When these boots go on sale, I'll be back in to get a pair."

He snorted and shook his head. "I don't care if you ever come back into this store again. Did I kill my girlfriend?" He shook his head. "You two are crazy."

"Oh, don't be that way. I need these boots," she said. When she had her shoes on, we hurried to the door.

"Better find them at another store then. You aren't welcome back here." He grabbed the box of boots and stomped to the backroom.

"That didn't go so well," Christy said when we were outside on the sidewalk.

"You think?" I asked her.

We had just made another mistake. Ethan was going to have a fit if he found out what we'd done.

Chapter Nineteen

WE STEPPED OUT ONTO the sidewalk and I turned back toward the candy store.

"Wait a minute, where are you going?" Christy asked.

I turned and looked at her. "Back to the candy store."

"Why? The clothing store is only two blocks away, and it's this direction," she said, nodding her head down the sidewalk in the opposite direction.

"Christy, we're not doing very well today. We practically accused two people of murder, and I'm reasonably sure that we were wrong. Actually, you did accuse Joey of murder. Besides, we've got to get back to work."

"What do you mean get back to work? We just eliminated two suspects. The odds are in our favor." She stubbornly crossed her arms in front of herself. It was cute, her being dressed as Dora.

I groaned. "Christy, Ethan's going to have a fit if we go down there and accuse Betty Mays of killing Hailey. Besides, she's mean. She isn't going to let us walk away if we're wrong."

"Now, we won't tell Ethan unless she really is the killer. Then we'll tell him and he can arrest her. He'll thank us for doing his job for him."

I looked at her incredulously. "Are you out of your mind? Ethan does not want us running around accusing people of murder."

She shrugged. "Possibly. But I'm also on the trail of a killer. Don't give up now. Good things come to those who wait."

"Good, let's wait for the police."

"Wait, that was the wrong idiom. It's supposed to be something about people who don't give up receive the prize. I know I heard something like that somewhere."

I chuckled. My sister could always make me laugh, but going after one more suspect today might be the death of us. Literally. "I think it's a bad idea."

"I know, I know. But look on the bright side. We could help put Hailey's killer behind bars. Justice is calling."

I may have thought it was a bad idea, but I walked with her down the street toward the clothing store anyway. What if it was true? What if Betty Mays really had killed Hailey Strong? Yes, we should have allowed the police to handle this, but the temptation to catch a killer was too great.

I sighed.

"Sometimes I like bad ideas," Christy confided as we walked.

"No, really?" I said sarcastically.

"Hard to believe, but true nonetheless."

My phone rang, and I pulled it from my pocket. It was Ethan. "Hey," I said answering it.

"Hey yourself. I saw I missed your call. What did you want?"

Uh-oh. Now I had to come up with a story. "Oh, I was just checking to see how you were. How are you?"

"I'm great. Still working on the case and hoping to have a break shortly."

I stopped. "You're hoping to have a break shortly? Like today?"

"Well, you never can tell when a break is going to present itself."

"Okay, so nothing definite."

Christy and I started walking down the sidewalk again.

"Wow, that's not very supportive," he said, chuckling. "What are you up to?"

"Right now? At this very moment?"

"Yes, right now at this very moment. Why are you talking like that?"

I shrugged, but of course, he couldn't see me over the phone. "I have a hunch about Betty Mays. What about the security cameras at the park? I know they don't point to the playground, but they do point to the parking lot, don't they?"

"Yeah, there are cameras on the parking lot. Why?"

"Who all came to the park that day that Hailey died?"

He chuckled. "Everyone. It was the two nights before the vendors' fair so there were the construction workers, people from the City Council, and lots and lots of vendors going to check out their booths. Why?"

"And Betty Mays? Was she there at the park?"

"We identified as many of the people as we could, but the cameras were set quite a distance from the parking lot and some people couldn't be identified. Why?"

We crossed the street and stood in front of the store next door to the clothing store. I didn't want Betty to catch sight of us standing in front of her store and get suspicious.

"Well, I believe Betty Mays may have killed Hailey. I think she was terrified that Hailey would tell her husband about the affair, and so she killed her to keep her mouth shut."

"I think that is a fair suspicion. And I've talked to her twice."

"So you don't think she's the killer?" I asked, disappointed.

"No, I didn't say that. I think it's a very good possibility that she is the killer, and I have my eye on her. Mia, what's going on? Tell me where you're at right now."

I took a deep breath. "Christy and I are standing in front of the store next to the dress shop."

"Why? What are you doing? You're not going to go in there and accuse her of murder are you?"

There was panic in his voice and I glanced at Christy, who put her hands up in the air in an attempt to let me know that she wanted to know what was going on.

"I talked to Joey Harper, and he says that Hailey got a call from Betty the day before we found her body. It was her day off, and she was annoyed that Betty was calling her at home. She wanted her to come to the park, to look at the booth they had been assigned."

Ethan was quiet for a moment. "Why didn't anyone tell me this?"

"Joey said he forgot and was going to call you and tell you about it."

There was a heavy sigh. "Mia, don't go in there. I'm going to come down there and have a talk with Betty."

"Okay, we'll wait for you."

"No, don't wait for me. Go back to the candy store. I'm sure there's lots of pumpkin spice fudge that you should be making."

"You're right. We'll be waiting for you." I hung up and turned to Christy.

"He's coming down here to talk to Betty. He warned us not to go into the store."

"And are we going to listen to him?"

I narrowed my eyes at her. "Yes, we're going to listen to him. Let's just hang out here and wait for a few minutes."

WE WERE STILL STANDING in front of the shop next door when Ethan pulled up and parked at the curb. He shook his head before he got out of the car and closed the door behind himself. "What are you two still doing here? I thought you had pumpkin spice fudge to make?"

I shrugged. "Yeah, we do. And we do need to get going, but we just thought we'd hang out in case Betty tried to make a break for it." I grinned at him and gave him a quick kiss. "You wouldn't want her to escape, would you?"

"Why would she try to escape if she didn't know she was under suspicion?"

I shrugged.

"We want to go in there with you," Christy said.

He shook his head. "No." And then he stopped and stared at a red sports car parked several spaces over. He walked over and stopped in front of the car.

"What's going on?" I asked, looking at the car.

"Somebody drove a car like this over to the parking lot at the park, but it was parked in the shade. I could tell it was red when it pulled into the parking lot, but because the driver got out of it in the shade, it was hard to tell who it was."

"If I'm not mistaken, that car belongs to Betty Mays," Christy said.

He turned and looked at her. Then he nodded. "You two get back to the candy store. Please. Don't make me take my badge out."

I looked at Christy, and she looked at me. "I don't want to go back to the candy store," she said.

"I don't want to argue with him, and I don't want him mad at us." I grabbed my sister by the hand, and I pulled her back down the sidewalk.

"Oh, come on, I don't want to miss this," she said, pulling back on my hand.

"You come on, I don't want to irritate Ethan," I said. "Besides, he'll tell us what happened."

I looked over my shoulder, and Ethan was entering the clothing store. I crossed my fingers in the hope that Hailey was going to get justice now.

Chapter Twenty

CHRISTY DROPPED A SUITCASE, a duffel bag, two pillows, and a blanket on my living room floor. "There. Welcome me home."

I chuckled. "Welcome home, Christy. At least, temporarily."

One eyebrow shot up. "What do you mean temporarily? I gave notice at my apartment. I have no place else to go."

"You know it's temporary. As soon as Ethan moves in with me, you're moving across the street."

"Oh good. I thought you changed your mind about having me as your roomie. I've got a few more things out in the car, and tomorrow I need you to help me take some boxes over to Mom and Dad's. Please."

"Sure, that's how I like to spend my days off," I said.

Devon appeared at the door with a cardboard box. "Hey, Mia."

I smiled. "Hey, Devon. Put that anywhere."

"You got it." He walked into the living room and set it next to Christy's other things.

"He's such a good boyfriend," Christy said and kissed him. He grinned.

"What do you two want for dinner? I bought a frozen lasagna, or we can order pizza. Or we can just have some cereal. It's hot, and I'm not in the mood to heat up the house by turning the oven on."

"We could go by someplace and pick something up," she offered. "I've got a few more things in the car. Come and help me get them out first."

Devon and I followed her out to her car that was parked behind mine at the curb. The car was stuffed with boxes and bags, two paintings, and clothing. "You don't travel lightly, do you?"

"No Way," Devon said and opened the back door.

She shook her head. "No. I hope you have a lot of closet space."

"Uh oh, that could be a problem," I said, reaching into the car and picking up a pile of shirts that were still on hangers. I folded them over one arm and reached into the car and picked up a small box.

"You might have to get rid of some of your stuff," she informed me as she picked up a big box out of the backseat.

"I don't know about that," I said. As we stood talking, Ethan pulled into his driveway across the street and parked. He got out of his truck and turned toward us.

"Well, if it isn't the nosy twins plus one," he called across the street.

"We aren't twins," I pointed out. Never mind the nosy part.

He chuckled and came across the street. "What are you three doing?"

"Christy is moving in with me. Remember?"

He nodded. "Yeah, I remember," he said.

"And if you're really a good brother-in-law, you could help us unload my car," Christy said as she carried the box up the sidewalk and into the house.

"I'm not technically her brother-in-law yet," Ethan grumbled and picked up another big box from the backseat.

"Doesn't matter, she'll put you to work," Devon said and picked up a box and carried it inside.

"Isn't it cute? She thinks of you as her brother-in-law. I think it's sweet." I said and carried the items in my hands up the sidewalk.

"It's lovely," he said.

It only took us another two trips to empty the car and bring everything into the house. I had hoped Christy would travel light, but I was wrong. I also hoped she wouldn't bring any of the other items from her apartment to my house. It was already cramped with what she had brought.

"So," I said and kissed Ethan. "What happened?"

He nodded. "She admitted to killing Hailey. Hailey had threatened her, saying she would tell her husband about the affair. And apparently, Hailey took a picture of the two of them with her phone before she approached her that day at the restaurant. So she had proof, and she said that she would show her husband if she didn't give her a raise. A huge raise."

"What a little sneak," Christy said and crashed on the couch. Devon sat next to her.

"Yeah, being a sneak can get you into trouble," Ethan said and sat down at the other end of the couch. I moved in and sat next to him.

"So it was planned, then?" Boo came and jumped on the couch and snuggled up in my lap.

"Yes, Betty saw the hole that had been dug near the playground equipment when she made her first trip to the park to check out her booth. That was earlier in the morning. Then she called Hailey and had her come later that evening. That's why everything was in the shadows, and I couldn't see who it was. It was hot that afternoon, so she had brought Hailey something to drink and put the sleeping pills in it. Then she busied her with wiping down the booth and asking her opinion on how they should set things up. The medication took about thirty minutes to kick in and she offered her a chair when she got drowsy." He reached over and pet Boo. "When Hailey dozed off, she dragged her over to the hole and filled it in by the cover of night."

"That's crazy," I said. "How did her barrettes end up on the ground like they did?"

"Betty said she had trouble dragging her to the hole. I figure Betty panicked when trying to drag her over to it, and she accidentally pulled them out of her hair."

I made a clucking sound and scratched Boo's ear. "What a shame. On both parts. If Hailey had just minded her own business and left things alone, she'd still be alive today."

"Yes, and if Betty wasn't so underhanded and had an affair on her husband, then decided to kill the only person that knew about it, or the only person she thought knew about it, she might still be alive," Ethan said.

I still didn't understand the business of murder. I just couldn't imagine a situation so drastic that I would feel like I had to kill someone. I leaned back on the couch and took Ethan's hand. I was glad the murder was solved, and we'd have more time together.

"Did you happen to bring home any of your mother's pumpkin spice fudge?" he asked.

I shook my head. "No. We sold out of it."

He leaned his head back. "That's a shame."

It truly was. I loved fudge, but especially pumpkin spice fudge. We were both addicted to it, and I wanted more of the tasty confection.

The End

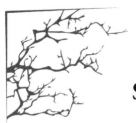

Sneak Peek

Pumpkin Spice Donuts and a Murder
A Rainey Daye Cozy Mystery, book 14

Chapter One

"Ready or not, here I come," I said, pushing the diner door open with my hip. I was carrying a huge tray of pumpkin cream cheese muffins and pumpkin spice donuts. I had to back in, trying to keep the tray from hitting the glass door. It was dark outside, and the diner's outside lights were all I had to see by.

My boss, Sam Stevens, hurried to my side and held the door for me so I could get through it without mishap. "Good morning, Rainey," he said with a nod. His eyes were glued to the tray in my hands. "What did you bring us?"

I grinned. "Pumpkin cream cheese muffins and pumpkin spice donuts. It's almost Halloween, and I'm so excited about it. I did some late night baking last night in anticipation of the big day."

"It's my favorite time of year," he said and followed me back to the kitchen. I was working the early shift at Sam's Diner, and I was a little bleary-eyed after having stayed up late the night before making the muffins and donuts. It was a spur of the moment thing, the idea having hit me much too late in the evening to stay up baking, but I did it anyway. When a great idea beckons, I've got to answer.

"Fall and Halloween are my favorite time of year, too," I said and set the tray down on the counter.

Our dishwasher, Ron White, turned to look at me. "Good morning, Rainey. Have I told you that you're one of my very favorite people in the entire world?" He came over and looked at the tray of goodies. It was covered in plastic wrap, and I could smell the spices through the wrapping.

I chuckled. "Wow, Ron, that's so sweet of you. You're one of my favorite people, too." I patted him on the shoulder. "Go ahead and help yourselves. I've been working on the recipes for a while, and I added lots and lots of spices. Let me know if I overdid it."

"I don't mind if I do," Sam said, unwrapping a corner of the tray and pulling out a pumpkin spice donut. "You know, this donut is the perfect breakfast food. It's got pumpkin for your veggies, the flour is your starch, and I bet there are eggs and milk for protein. Am I right, Rainey?"

I nodded. "You are right. And I agree with you, it's the perfect breakfast food. I'm going to get the coffee started. We have a few minutes to enjoy a donut or a muffin with some coffee before we open."

I hurried over to the industrial-sized coffee maker that was behind the front counter and got started on the coffee. I glanced around the dark dining room and shrugged. It had been a few months since one of our waitresses had been murdered. There were days that I felt sure she was lurking around the corners of the diner. Silly, I know. But she had been a waitress at the diner since before I had begun working here, and now she was gone. Even though we hadn't gotten along, it felt wrong somehow.

It only took a moment to put the coffee and the water into the machine, and I stood back and waited, inhaling the scent of freshly brewing coffee. There were few things I enjoyed more in the morning than fresh coffee with a tasty baked good.

I could hardly wait to get off work. It was October, the leaves on the trees were turning, and I intended to enjoy these last weeks of wonderful weather before it turned to snow. Taking my dog Maggie for a walk in the woods was on my list of things to do this afternoon.

I glanced up when a dark figure came to the diner door. I hesitated for a moment, then realized it was my boyfriend, Detective Cade Starkey. Hurrying over to the door, I unlocked it and let him inside, and locked it behind him again.

"Good morning," he said with a grin and leaned over and kissed me.

"Good morning, yourself," I said and kissed him back. "I've got coffee brewing, and I made pumpkin cream cheese muffins and pumpkin spice donuts. How does that sound for breakfast?"

He nodded and grinned again. "Are you kidding me? That sounds like the perfect breakfast, and the coffee smells great. And boy, do I need some."

"You better get a cup before you die from a lack of caffeine," I said and headed back behind the front counter. "There's nothing like a fresh cup of coffee."

"It's a little dark in here," he said, glancing around.

I chuckled and flipped the light switch on, and the dining room was illuminated. "We just walked in the door a few minutes ago, and I guess we forgot to turn the lights on."

He nodded as I got him a cup and poured the coffee while it was still brewing, then handed it to him. "You know where the cream and sugar are."

"I certainly do," he said and went back to the kitchen to help himself.

I poured three more cups of coffee and set the pot back beneath the coffee maker. I balanced the cups, two in one hand, and one in the other, and brought them to the kitchen. "Here we are." I set the cups down next to the tray of muffins and donuts and saw that Cade already had a pumpkin muffin in his hand. "You don't waste any time, do you?"

He shook his head and chuckled. "Are you kidding me? You said there were pumpkin muffins, and I couldn't risk letting everybody else eat them all before I got one."

"You on your way to work, Cade?" Sam asked as he picked up one of the cups of coffee and poured cream into it.

Cade nodded. "When I passed by, I saw Rainey's car parked in the parking lot. There was no way I could drive by without stopping to say hello." He winked at me.

"Good thing you did," Ron said, picking up a pumpkin donut. "You might have missed out on these tasty treats."

"Right?" Cade said and took another bite of his muffin.

I turned to Cade. "So where are you going to take me this weekend?"

His brow furrowed. "Was I supposed to take you someplace?"

I rolled my eyes. "Of course you were supposed to take me someplace. It's the weekend."

"But today's only Tuesday," he pointed out and took another bite of his muffin. "This is really good, Rainey." He glanced at the rest of the muffins on the tray.

"Thank you. And I'm thinking ahead. It's fall, the weather is beautiful, and the leaves are dropping from the trees. I just want to go someplace. I don't know where, but let's get out of town and enjoy the beautiful scenery."

One eyebrow shot up. "You mean you want to go fishing? Fishing is an outdoor activity, and we can watch the leaves dropping from the trees."

I narrowed my eyes at him. "I did not say I wanted to go fishing. Get that idea out of your mind."

"Why would I get that idea out of my mind?" he asked innocently. "The earthworms are crawling, and just begging to be put on a hook. Stinky marshmallows need to be put on a hook, too."

Sam chuckled. "It's quite magnanimous of those earthworms."

"Yes well, they insist on helping me catch the biggest trout in the lake. What am I going to do about it?"

Sam chuckled and headed toward the kitchen door. "I think it's about time to open the doors. I hate to break that to all of you, but it's six o'clock."

I groaned. I needed to get some more caffeine inside of me if I was going to make it through the breakfast shift. With the weather being as lovely as it was, we were still fairly busy even though the summer tourist season had ended. There were still a lot of tourists that came during the fall to go fishing and camping, and just enjoy the beautiful weather.

"I guess if you have to, you have to," I said, but he had already left the kitchen.

Cade drank some of his coffee and set the cup down. "I really should get going, but I hate to leave." He leaned over and kissed me again.

"Let me get you a to-go cup for your coffee, and you can take a couple of these muffins and donuts with you to work. How does that sound?"

"That sounds excellent," he said. I wrapped up two muffins and two donuts, handed them to him, and we headed back out front.

"See you later, Ron," Cade said over his shoulder.

"See you later, Cade."

I poured Cade's coffee into a paper cup, then added more from the pot to top it off, and put a lid on it. I handed it to him and he smiled. "Well, I guess if you have to go to work, you have to go to work. But I'll miss you."

He grinned and leaned across the front counter and kissed me. "I'll miss you, too. I'll give you a call later."

I nodded and watched him turn and head out of the diner. Then I glanced down at the promise ring on my hand. Cade wanted to exchange that promise ring for an engagement ring, and I was halfway ready to let him. But the specter of my failed marriage still popped up in the corners of my mind from time to time.

I looked up as Bernie Jones and Fred Binkley walked through the diner door. I smiled at them. "Hello fellas, how are you this morning?"

Fred waved a hand at me. "I guess I'm all right, Rainey. It's going to be a pretty day, but I'm not looking forward to the winter. My lumbago is due to kick in any time now."

"Oh, you're always grumbling," Bernie said and chuckled. "How are you doing, Rainey?"

I nodded. "I'm doing great, Bernie. Can I get you both some coffee to start?"

Fred nodded, and they both took a seat at the front counter. "Coffee sounds great."

I headed over to the coffee maker and poured two cups of coffee and brought it back and set it down in front of them. "I've got some pumpkin muffins and donuts in the kitchen. Any interest in those?"

Fred's eyes got big. "I would love a pumpkin muffin. Haven't had one of those in a long while."

I nodded. "You got it. What about you, Bernie?"

Bernie grabbed a menu from off the counter and looked it over. "All that sounds great, Rainey, but my blood sugar has just been too high lately, and my wife has been on my case about it. I better stick with some protein."

"Well, I can't blame you for that," I said and pulled out an order book and a pen from my apron pocket and got their ticket started.

The beginning of a new day. There was something about it that I enjoyed. The day was full of promise, and that promise would bring something good with it. Right?

IF YOU'D LIKE UPDATES on the newest books I'm writing, follow me on Amazon and Facebook:

https://www.facebook.com/
Kathleen-Suzette-Kate-Bell-authors-759206390932120/

https://www.amazon.com/Kathleen-Suzette/e/
B07B7D2S4W/ref=dp_byline_cont_pop_ebooks_1

Made in United States
North Haven, CT
14 March 2022

17157752R00088